Darcy didn't get to he

Not that she wasn't ready a...
They quivered as if she'd run all day. She ignored Blake waiting at the door, ready to take off. She wasn't about to chance falling on her face at the feet of this overbearing man who remained oblivious to her shock at his appearance.

This. . .this fully grown man was the boy who'd stolen her father's affections? She'd excused her father all these years by imagining the boy he'd chosen to raise as his own when he married his second wife was a cute little toddler while Darcy was already a gangly adolescent. That neatly explained why her father didn't want anything to do with her. But this man had to be older than she. It shot her theory to the mountain peaks and back.

And for no one to let her know she had a little sister? To hide the fact of Darcy's existence from the girl, as if she—Darcy—could be erased from all of their lives?

It was unforgivable. Her stomach coiled and twisted. She couldn't believe no one had said anything. Not one word. It couldn't be more obvious that she'd intentionally been shut out.

What did she expect? It had always been the same. Her father never thought of her. Even this inheritance promised to be one colossal headache. She hadn't wanted to come to this meeting. In fact, she'd sooner have stood on hot coals in her bare feet, thank you very much. But the lawyer hadn't given her an option, so she'd driven almost a thousand miles to be here.

Blake rattled the doorknob. "Ready?"

LINDA FORD and her husband raised a family of fourteen children, ten adopted, providing her plenty of opportunities to experience God's love and faithfulness. One of her goals in writing is to reveal a little of God's wondrous love through the lives of the people in her stories. She lives in Alberta, Canada, on a ranch she shares with her husband, a paraplegic client, boomerang children, and adorable visiting grandchildren.

Books by Linda Ford

HEARTSONG PRESENTS
HP240—The Sun Still Shines
HP268—Unchained Hearts
HP368—The Heart Seeks a Home
HP448—Chastity's Angel
HP463—Crane's Bride
HP531—Lizzie
HP547—Maryelle
HP575—Grace
HP599—Irene
HP614—Forever In My Heart
HP701—Cry of My Heart

Darcy's Inheritance

Linda Ford

Heartsong Presents

A note from the Author:
I love to hear from my readers! You may correspond with me by writing:

Linda Ford
Author Relations
PO Box 721
Uhrichsville, OH 44683

ISBN 978-1-59789-294-0

DARCY'S INHERITANCE

Our mission is to publish and distribute inspirational products offering exceptional value and biblical encouragement to the masses.

PRINTED IN THE U.S.A.

one

Late. Again. Blake Thompson rushed into the house and headed for his bedroom. How long did it take to read a will? How long to settle things amicably and shake hands all around so he could get back to his chores? Cows and calves to look after. The tractor to service. He didn't have time for this, but he had too much at stake to avoid it. He breathed a silent prayer: *Lord, let this be short and sweet.*

He grabbed his wallet and headed down the hall, his six-year-old half sister, Amy, dogging his heels.

"How long you going to be gone?"

"Not a minute longer than I have to."

"I wish I could go. There's nothin' to do here."

He paused at the living room. "Aunt Betty!" he called to the older woman sitting across the room. "I'm on my way to town. Anything you need?" She shook her head as she concentrated on her knitting.

"I wanna go with you," Amy persisted.

"You'd just have to sit in the truck. Besides, don't you have twelve cats waiting to play with you?" The cats were a nuisance, always underfoot in the supply room, but he wouldn't deny his sister the pleasure she got from her pets.

"Can you get me more cat food?"

"Hey, aren't you afraid they'll get fat and lazy?" He grinned down at her. "And then they wouldn't do their job."

Her gorgeous blue eyes could be dark and moody one moment, and the next, guileless and sky bright, like now. "Uh-uh." She shook her head until her blond hair sprayed around her face. "Bullet caught a mouse yesterday. He's real

5

fast, you know." She stuck out her bottom lip. "You never take me with you."

Ignoring her whining, he held out his arms. "Come on. Give your big brother a hug and kiss." He braced himself as she launched into his arms, squeezing her arms around his neck until he could hardly breathe.

He slowly released her, letting her land on his boots. She clung to him, giggling when he swung her high with each step until he reached the truck. "Gotta go, squirt. Behave yourself while I'm gone."

Twenty minutes later he jerked to a halt on the main street of Blissdale, Montana, population 786. For a moment he rested his forearms on the steering wheel. His own father had died when he was thirteen, and his mother four years ago. He still missed them. Sure, he didn't think about them all the time; but when he least expected it, *pow*—a sucker punch jerked his breath away. He knew it wouldn't be any different with Rob.

He straightened, rolled up his sleeves, hung his sunglasses from his breast pocket, and slid from his truck. He dusted the seat of his jeans and strode past the sign—EUGENE SMART, BARRISTER AND SOLICITOR—and into the office. Gene's receptionist ushered him into the inner room.

She sat across the desk from the lawyer—the woman who'd refused to visit Rob as he lay dying.

But she sure had no trouble making it to the reading of the will.

He'd seen Rob's photo of her as a kid and knew she bore a resemblance to Amy. He just wasn't prepared for how strong the likeness was. Clear blue eyes like his little sister's. And right now they were cool and steady. In fact, if he didn't miss his guess, he would say they were challenging. As if daring him to object to her presence. Fiery, red-hot lights burst in his head. He objected, all right.

He stared hard, intending to let her know what he thought about her dereliction of duty. The way he looked at it, if a person didn't have normal affection, he or she still had duty. This woman had neither. She deserved nothing of Rob's.

She wore a denim skirt and black high-heeled boots. He focused for a moment on the boots. On any other woman he might have thought them attractive.

Gene stood. "Miss Hagen, let me introduce Blake Thompson."

The woman held out her hand. "Hello."

Tall and slender with a voice of pure music. Too bad the music didn't go any deeper than her voice box.

Blake hesitated, then took her cool, smooth fingers. He resisted an urge to jerk back and shove his large, rough hands in his pockets. He withdrew slowly and faced Gene. "Let's get this finished. I have things to do."

Gene nodded him toward a chair, then looked at her. "Are you ready to proceed, Miss Hagen?"

"Yes, let's get this over with." She settled back and crossed her legs.

Blake stared at the books crowding the shelves behind Gene. He caught a whiff of orange. Wasn't much chance it came from Gene's dusty books and stacks of papers.

The lawyer rustled the papers before him. "Rob was very clear and specific about the terms of his will." He gave Blake a steady look, then ducked his head and read, "I hereby bequeath to Blake Thompson my share of the land and all farm-type assets." The lawyer glanced up. "He knew the ranch morally belonged to you even though your mother had made him joint owner when they married."

Blake nodded. Better than what he'd expected. He crossed one ankle over his knee and tried not to think of the chores left to do.

"Exclusive," Gene read, "of what is known as the 'old property' consisting of five acres and a house, which I bequeath to my daughter Darcy Hagen." He smiled at Darcy. "There are two houses on the ranch. The older one has its own title, and it's now yours."

Blake dropped both feet to the floor and faced *Miss Hagen*. "I knew Rob would leave you something. Just wasn't sure what. I've already made arrangements for the necessary funds to purchase the property from you. We can sign the papers now, and I'll transfer the money to your account as soon as everything clears."

She looked remote, as if none of this meant anything to her. But of course it didn't. She hadn't wanted anything to do with the ranch or its inhabitants when her father was alive. And he, Blake Thompson, now owner of the entire spread except for a few acres, didn't want anything to do with her. She had no part of his home, his life, or his thoughts.

She returned his stare with clear blue eyes, not flinching before his displeasure. He always got a kick out of the way Amy fearlessly tried to stare him down when she was in trouble, but the same look from this woman made his neck muscles twitch.

"How much money are we talking about?" she asked.

"Fair market value."

She slid her gaze away but not before he saw her silent accusation and the quirk of her eyebrows, her message as plain as the barlike rays of sunshine slanting through the blinds beside Gene's desk. *As if I'd trust you.* He resisted the urge to grind his teeth.

"I'll let you handle the details of the sale," she told *his* lawyer, then uncrossed her legs and leaned back. "I have no interest in anything my father left me. We've had no contact for years. How long will it take? I have obligations back home."

Gene rattled some papers. "I think you'd both better listen to the rest of the will before you make any decisions." He took a deep breath. "Your father named you both as joint guardians of Amy."

Blake's mouth dropped open. He clamped it shut, swallowed hard, and found a croaky imitation of his voice. "No way."

Gene ignored his protest as he focused on *that* woman.

Darcy leaned forward. He was sure he could hear the gears turning in her head. *Is this going to interfere with my plans to take the money and run?* "Who is Amy?"

Gene ricocheted a glance off Blake, then kept his gaze on Darcy. "Amy is your half sister. Your father and Blake's mother had a child. Your father's wife passed away four years ago, so Amy is now without parents. Luckily she has two siblings. You and Blake."

"I have a sister?" Her voice spiraled upward. She spun around and glared at Blake. "Why didn't anyone tell me?"

He let her see his scorn. "In this part of the country, the telephone lines run both ways."

Her Amy-blue eyes turned icy. "In my part of the country, so do the mail, the airplanes, and the roads."

Gene sighed loudly. "Can we get back to the business at hand? There are decisions to be made."

Blake corralled his desire to yank the will from the lawyer's hands and shred it. "What decisions? Nothing's changed as far as I'm concerned. I'll pay her for the piece of land she inherited, and she can get back to her life."

"You'll have to sign custody agreement documents. You'll need to—"

Blake slapped his hand against his thigh. "I won't be signing any such thing. Gene, make out the papers for the purchase of the land. Call me when everything's in order." He strode across the room.

"This changes everything." Her words stopped him as if he'd run into a fence. "I want to meet my little sister."

He slowly turned around. "Over my dead body."

Gene stood. "Blake, she has a right—"

Blake scowled at Gene. "As far as I'm concerned, she has no

right." He glowered at the woman, his eyes burning.

She pressed the tips of her fingers together in a tent. "It wouldn't have hurt anyone to tell me about her. Does she know about me?"

Blake shook his head. "Rob thought it would only confuse her."

The coldhearted woman planted both feet on the floor. "I'd like to see this house I've inherited and my little sister."

"What happened to your obligations?"

Her triumphant smile grated up his spine. "Your lawyer warned me I might need a few days to take care of business, so I took some time off. I meant to spend it touring the mountains, but I can delay my trip for a few days."

Gene must have noticed the way Blake clenched and unclenched his jaw and curled his fists into knots. "Blake, what's the harm? Take her out to the ranch. Show her the house. Introduce Amy." He paused. "I'm sorry, but you really don't have a choice."

Frustration gnawed at Blake's throat. He prayed for patience, knowing he was going to need more than the usual amount. "How many are a few days?"

She shrugged and smiled. "I'm free for the next two weeks."

He didn't welcome two days. Not even two hours. Two weeks? No way. "What about your vacation in the mountains?"

"I'm uncommitted."

"No kidding."

"To a schedule."

"Then it's settled." Gene tidied the papers on his desk in obvious relief. "I'm sure Blake will be glad to show you to the ranch."

Blake choked back a growl. He'd be glad to show her the way out of town. *Lord, where is that patience I ordered?*

"I'm sure I can get directions from Gene," she said in a smooth, cool voice.

Gene shot him a warning look.

Blake knew when he was over a barrel. "Forget it. I'll show you the way."

⊱

Darcy didn't get to her feet right away. Not that she wasn't ready and willing—except for her legs. They quivered as if she'd run all day. She ignored Blake waiting at the door, ready to take off. She wasn't about to chance falling on her face at the feet of this overbearing man who remained oblivious to her shock at his appearance.

This. . .this fully grown man was the boy who'd stolen her father's affections? She'd excused her father all these years by imagining the boy he'd chosen to raise as his own when he married his second wife was a cute little toddler while Darcy was already a gangly adolescent. That neatly explained why her father didn't want anything to do with her. But this man had to be older than she. It shot her theory to the mountain peaks and back.

And for no one to let her know she had a little sister? To hide the fact of Darcy's existence from the girl as if she— Darcy—could be erased from all of their lives?

It was unforgivable. Her stomach coiled and twisted. She couldn't believe no one had said anything. Not one word. It couldn't be more obvious that she'd intentionally been shut out.

What did she expect? It had always been the same. Her father never thought of her. Even this inheritance promised to be one colossal headache. She hadn't wanted to come to this meeting. In fact, she'd sooner have stood on hot coals in her bare feet, thank you very much. But the lawyer hadn't given her an option, so she'd driven almost a thousand miles to be here.

Blake rattled the doorknob. "Ready?"

"You bet." She picked up her tiny purse. While pretending to adjust the straps, she gave her limbs a desperate command.

Don't fail me now. She could do this. It was like preparing for a race. She took a deep breath and held it until oxygen flowed to her muscles. "Thank you, Mr. Smart." She could spare the time to be polite to the lawyer. And use the delay to steady herself.

She pushed from the chair and tested her legs, breathing easier when they held her weight. But she reached for the edge of the lawyer's desk as quivering trembled up her body and settled in her stomach. She wasn't going to throw up, was she?

"What are you driving?"

"A car." When he sighed, she added, "The little red one at the curb." He didn't need to look at her as if she'd left her brain in storage. Her state of shock was his fault, after all. His and her father's. It required a miracle for her to walk after the information dumped on her.

She followed the glowering man outside. It didn't take a genius to see Blake Thompson wasn't pleased with the way the reading of the will had gone.

Ha! He ought to try being in her shoes. She glanced down at her footwear. Or boots. She stood at the curb, staring at her car. "I have a little sister." She thought she wouldn't talk to him at all, but the words slipped out. In fact, a whole crowd of words rushed to her mouth. "Her name's Amy?"

Blake faced her, his expression hard. "Listen to me. Amy doesn't need you. She's well cared for and happy. And you don't need her. You've made that obvious."

She planted her booted feet several inches apart and stuck her face close to his, raising to her tiptoes to help equalize their height. "You know nothing about me, so you can stop judging me. And you can just accept the fact that I am going to see my house and meet my sister." She settled back on her heels. "Like it or live with it. I don't care."

He muttered something nasty under his breath.

Like that hurt. "I've never owned a house. Never lived in

one of our own growing up. I might like it so much I'll decide to stay." She enjoyed goading him, especially when his eyes turned thunderous. "I'm really looking forward to meeting Amy. How old did you say she was?"

His long legs ate up the distance to a big black truck complete with dual wheels and roll bar. "I didn't."

And you don't intend to. "Fine. I like surprises." Nice surprises like a party, a great sale, a new flavor of coffee that purred across her tongue. She could well do without the sort of surprise Blake Thompson was turning out to be. Seeing him had shaken her far worse than she cared to think possible. Why had her father chosen him over her? She shook her head and shoved back the anger tearing at her throat. And a little sister? Not only had she been robbed of her father, but she'd also been robbed of a sister. She closed her eyes. *Lord, help me remember the past is forgiven. Help me not let it steal away my joy.* She opened her eyes and smiled into the blue sky.

"Get in your car if you want to follow me to the ranch."

She jerked her heels together and saluted. "Yes, sir." At the look of outrage darkening his face before he yanked open the truck door, she laughed. No way was she going to let him get on her nerves. Even as she thought it, a pain shafted up the side of her face, and she reminded herself to relax her jaw.

"I have to stop at the grocery store." His tone indicated she could follow him or rot in the sunshine. And she knew which he preferred.

"Good idea. I'll need some supplies if I'm going to enjoy living in *my* house."

The slam of his door shook the truck. The motor growled to life, and he roared away from the curb.

She followed him down the dusty little street, her mind spinning as fast as the wheels under her car. "I have a little sister." Over and over she repeated the words, trying to get her head around the idea. Shivers raced up her arms. A sister.

She tried to picture her, but not knowing if the child was big or little or somewhere in between made it impossible. She did some quick mental arithmetic. Her sister had to be at least four given the fact Blake's mother died that long ago. When had she last spoken to her father? She pretended to think about the answer. But she remembered very well. Seven years ago after he'd failed to show up for her high school graduation.

So many times she'd built fantasies of his return. After his marriage to Blake's mom, she had dreamed of visits. She waited for him on her birthdays even though she had no reason to think he'd come. No reason but her own need. Each time he failed to show, she made excuses for him. Too far. Too busy. Forgot.

But missing her graduation hurt. This time he had promised. She'd counted on it, planned on it for weeks. And then for every one of her friends to witness her disappointment. . .

That's when she'd made the decision she wouldn't give him the opportunity to disappoint her again.

Had she had a little sister then? Would her father have bothered to tell her if she had?

Fifteen years ago he'd married Blake's mother. Maybe her father chose this family over her because Amy was on the way. Not because Blake was a cute toddler.

That meant Amy would be fifteen.

Or not. No one had ever said a word about it. Not even Mom. She gripped the steering wheel so hard her fingers cramped. A combination of surprise and anger—fresh and hot—stung her insides, uncovering an old, old sense of being so unimportant in her father's eyes she became invisible.

Blake pulled to a stop in front of a building with a plain brown face of aluminum siding and a bold black-and-white sign across the entire front: BROWN'S GENERAL STORE.

Darcy parked beside Blake's truck. She took a moment to push away the turmoil inside her and whispered another prayer. "Please, God. I've dealt with those feelings. With Your help I've put them to rest. Please help me concentrate on all the good things You've given me." She smiled hard. *Like a sister.* She couldn't wait to meet this surprise person. It was the most incredible thing—she had a sister. She *was* a sister. They were about to meet for the first time. A little thrill skittered up her spine. All her life she'd felt isolated by her father's leaving. Sure, she had Mom, but somehow it never seemed she had family. But a sister made her part of a nuclear family unit. Sort of. She could hardly wait to meet her.

No way Darcy could express to her sister how much it meant to have someone, but she'd take a gift of welcome and gratitude.

Oh, yeah, and she'd see the house her father willed her. What would it look like? The old property, the lawyer said. Probably a decrepit building. Probably short in modernization. She wrinkled her nose. Would there be an outhouse?

Unless the toilet stood white—or any color but wood—and flushable in a room with a tub and a sink, she'd be heading straight back to town and the comfort of a motel. She glanced around. She didn't see a motel, but she'd find one.

Not that she planned to stay long. She'd meet her little sister, decide what to do about her guardianship responsibilities, and sell the house as Blake had suggested. She snorted. His "suggestion" sounded more like an order. Not that it mattered. She wanted nothing to do with the hurtful emotions she associated with her father or Blake's obvious displeasure.

Blake disappeared into the store, and she hurried after him, catching him just inside the door.

"I'd like to take Amy a gift." She spoke to the man's back because he left her no choice.

He seemed bent on putting as much distance between them as possible. "It would help to know how old she is and what she likes."

A young man with a nose too big for his face stood behind the counter. He glanced up from reading a magazine. "Hey, Blake!" he called. "How's it going?"

"Hi, Joe. Things are just great." Darcy knew she didn't imagine the sarcasm in his voice. He turned to her. "Listen to me. Amy doesn't need anything. Get it? Nothing."

Darcy hoped she revealed only her stubbornness. "I'd have to be as stupid as this cart"—she yanked one toward her—"not to 'get it.' You want me to know Amy doesn't need me." As if he had to say it. How much more obvious could it be than to keep Amy's existence a secret? "But need I remind you that apparently my father thought differently?" A little late in the game, but at least he'd remembered her in death, if not in life.

Blake spun around and strode down an aisle.

She headed in a different direction. Halfway down the length of the store she remembered to look at the shelves for supplies. Suddenly she stared ahead. The modern grocery store at the front had become an old-fashioned hardware store with coffee-colored wooden shelves and creaky oiled wood floors complete with the scent of lemon oil, twine, and leather. She wanted to linger, poke through the shelves and touch pieces of history, but she heard Blake back at the cash register. She grabbed items off the shelves. She'd need some food if she meant to stay at the house, and she selected fresh produce.

Blake stood at the checkout with a super-big bag of cat food. She wondered if he had a super-big cat to match.

She stood in front of the household section, shamelessly listening to the conversation between Blake and the clerk as she decided what she needed. Definitely some cleaners and a good strong bug killer. She put an extra-large, industrial-strength can of it in her cart.

The young man at the counter chuckled. "More food for Amy's cats?"

Blake laughed, too. "Gonna have to take on a part-time job just to pay for cat food."

Cats, huh? She detoured down the next aisle and selected a handful of cat toys. Not exactly her top choice for the first gift for a new sister. But better than twine and nails.

As she unloaded her cart to ring her selections through, Blake waited at the door, glancing frequently at his watch and casting a look toward his truck as if trying to decide if he should wait or leave her to find her own way to the ranch.

"What brings you to our part of the country?" the clerk asked.

She ignored Blake's impatient sigh. "I've come to see the house I inherited."

The young man raised his eyebrows and glanced at Blake, who said in a voice thick with resignation, "Rob's daughter, Darcy. She inherited the old house."

She certainly didn't like the way they kept saying "old house" and shuddered at visions of huge spiders. Fat, lazy mice. Spooky sounds in the walls. Maybe she should get another can of bug killer.

The young man leaned over the counter. "Welcome to your new home. My name's Joe Brown."

She smiled at the eager clerk as she scooped up the bagged groceries and rushed after Blake. "Wait. How far is it? When can I meet Amy? We need to talk."

He brushed at his face as if she were a pesky mosquito. "If you follow me, I'll take you to your house." He headed for the truck as if a national emergency required his immediate attention.

Darcy called after him, again talking to the man's back. "I *will* be meeting my sister," she said, her voice hard with determination. "You don't have the right to refuse it."

He yanked the door open and spun around. "The way I see it, a piece of paper written by a dying man doesn't give you the right to march in here and start making demands."

She took a step toward him. "That piece of paper gives me as much right as you. And I will not be denied it." She'd been pushed out, left in the dark, excluded from her rights as a daughter all her life. She would not let anyone, including Blake Thompson, keep her away from her sister.

Blake yanked his truck door shut, effectively shutting out any more discussion.

Darcy clenched her teeth as she crawled into her car, depositing her purchases on the seat beside her. No way was he going to deny her access to her sister.

two

Darcy followed Blake down the highway. As the road flashed under her wheels, she looked about. The Rockies rose in the west like uneven dinosaur teeth. She'd loved the drive through the mountains, the sun shining off them so gloriously. She imagined herself running down the highway, breathing in the rare air, waving to the deer in the trees. By the time she got back to Seattle she'd be in such great condition she'd easily win the charity challenge run. She, Darcy Hagen, the winner, pumping her arms over her head in a victory cheer and everyone from her office yelling and congratulating her. As the winner, her office would present the funds raised by the event to the charity of its choice—the homeless shelter.

She smiled at the thought. Maybe the homeless wouldn't be off the streets, but at least they'd have a place to sleep.

Now she didn't know if she'd be spending much time in the mountains. She wanted to meet Amy and get to know her. Anger spurted to the surface again. How would she ever make up for the missed years, be they four or fifteen?

She sucked in a deep steadying breath and prayed for peace in her heart. Slowly her anger abated, and she returned her attention to the sights outside the car.

Grassy fields spread out like thick, pale gold corduroy. Other fields seemed thin, as if they'd been washed too often—some kind of crop residue from the last growing season, she guessed. But what she knew about farming or ranching wouldn't fill the cap of her pen. Cows she recognized and knew they came in various colors, mostly brown and black.

The brake lights flashed in the monster truck ahead of her,

and she slowed as Blake turned onto a gravel road. His dust forced her to drop back, but she didn't have to worry about getting lost. The swirling gray cloud shouted the way.

A few minutes later the air cleared as Blake pulled to a stop. She glanced at her watch. Twenty minutes from town. Unbelievable. She couldn't imagine not being able to run across the street for a magazine or to the corner for a mocha.

As she parked next to his truck, her gaze riveted on the small house behind him. Her house? She couldn't imagine owning a house. Too bad it was out in the middle of Nowhere, Montana. She leaned over the steering wheel and peered through the window. It didn't look *that* old. Sure, the trim needed painting, and a curtain hung crookedly in one window. But it had a sunporch. Just like a summer home. A place where a person could come and forget her troubles. Her insides ping-ponged around. A haven.

Not that she needed a physical haven. Years ago she'd found what she needed in her faith. One of her favorite verses caressed her thoughts. It was from Deuteronomy—chapter thirty-three, if she remembered correctly. *"The eternal God is your refuge, and underneath are the everlasting arms."* Her faith had sustained her for years and would continue to do so into the future. She took a deep breath and let peace fill her mind.

Her attention turned to Blake, shifting from foot to foot and frowning so deeply he drove gouges into his forehead. She sighed. Looks as if she might need a haven, after all— someplace to get away from him. She gave him a little wave and laughed at his curt nod, refusing to let his bad temper steal away her stubborn peace.

She studied him. How would she describe him to the girls at the office? Rude.

And physically? She examined him closely, building a word picture. Lean, like a runner. All muscle. Long legs and broad shoulders. She studied his face. Wide forehead. Nicely shaped brows. Short brown hair brushed back. Highlighted with blond streaks, straight from sunny Mother Nature, if she didn't miss her guess. Irene would sigh dramatically if she could see his eyes. Dark brown and intense. In fact, to be honest, if he were anyone but her father's stepson, she'd be just a tiny bit interested in him.

He crossed his arms and glowered at her.

She blinked. How long had she been staring at the poor guy? She hurried to get out of the car. As she straightened, she plastered on a smile. "This is my house?" A bouquet of strange scents greeted her—pungent animal smells, the aroma of damp, sweet hay, and the hint of something sharp and spicy.

He nodded. "Give me a couple of minutes to clean out some stuff." He pulled a box from the truck and headed to the door.

Darcy bounced after him. "Listen—we have to discuss Amy. When am I going to meet her?"

He threw open the door without answering.

"It wasn't locked?" She hesitated, glancing around nervously. They stood in an entryway large enough for a washer and dryer and a row of hooks holding an assortment of Goodwill coats. "What if someone's in here?"

"There's a key on the nail by the door if you want to keep it locked."

A sigh released her lungs. "That's good." But he'd already stepped into the next room. She hurried after him to a large, airy kitchen. A wooden table and mismatched chairs stood in one corner next to patio doors with a view of the sunroom. She could almost imagine settling in, stretched out on a chaise lounge, reading and enjoying the sunshine. Her skin warmed. She could hardly wait. She even had a recent fashion magazine. This could be enjoyable if she didn't have to contend with Blake and his lack of cooperation.

"You can't keep ignoring me. I have a right—"

Blake picked up a shirt and a clock and dumped them in the box.

"Someone's living here?" In her shock and excitement she hadn't thought she might be putting someone out of their home. "Who?"

"No one lives here." He crossed to the next room.

Darcy followed him into what was the living room—a fireplace at one end, dusty bookshelves across another wall. It looked and felt occupied. "Sure looks like someone lives here." She faltered. "I wouldn't make them leave. I can always go back to town and stay in a motel."

"I said no one lives here. Besides, it's yours. Remember?" As he talked he carefully took some framed photos off the shelves.

Peering past him, she saw a serene-looking woman standing beside a familiar figure. "That's my father."

He dropped the photo into the box.

"Was that your mother with him?" she asked.

"Uh-huh."

"Did they live here?" Getting words out of this man was like trying to gain an extra minute in an hour.

"No. They lived in the new house."

"Then why is their picture here?"

He picked up a trophy of a man swinging a rope and set it in the box before he faced her. "I lived here until. . . " He turned away but not before she'd seen the tightness around his eyes. "Until Rob got sick and I moved in with them to help."

Darcy's thoughts stuttered. She didn't want to think about her father.

"Rob lived here before he and Mom married," Blake said.

Something cold dribbled down Darcy's spine. Her father lived here at a time when she still hoped he'd come back to her and her mother. When she still believed things would work out. She spun away and stared out the window, forcing herself to see the view. Mountains far to the west. Dark brooding pines to the right. Scraggy-fingered poplars to the left. "How long was he sick?" She hadn't meant to say the words. She hadn't even meant to think them. No way was she going to give the past any power in her life.

"Almost a year."

"I'm sorry. Truly I am. It must have been a difficult time for you."

His gaze scorched her.

Instinctively she stepped back and raised her hands to protect her face from the heat.

"How can it mean nothing to you?"

"Look. I said I'm sorry about your loss. I know it's recent and still hurts like mad. I got over my loss years ago."

He made a choking sound as he grabbed his box and strode into the next room. She sighed deeply. Maybe she should turn around and go back to town. Only she had a little sister she was truly curious about. So she followed Blake into a sunny room he'd obviously used as an office. The large oak desk would have held his computer. There remained a stack of paper in a tray and mugs filled with pens and pencils.

He stood in the middle of the room. "I slept here as a kid. Before my parents built the new house." He wandered over to the window and stared out.

His silence made Darcy uncomfortable. She didn't want to be dragged into his grief.

Suddenly he faced her, his expression dark. "He was a wonderful father to me."

Her heart clenched. Pain shot through her chest. His words stung. But it wasn't as if she'd never before thought what it meant that her father raised someone else's child.

She could deal with her unexpected reaction. It was no different from running. You hit a spot where you wanted to give up. Your muscles hurt. Your lungs screamed for air. But you pushed past that hurdle, and suddenly it eased. Your lungs learned to expand. Your muscles got the required oxygen, and you settled into a rhythm you could maintain for miles. She just had to focus on her breathing until it leveled. She sucked in air and eased it out slowly.

His expression had softened as if he'd read her reaction, but she didn't want to hear another word about her father. Giving him a curt nod, she said, "How nice for you." The room suddenly crowded in on her, and she hurried away.

She peeked into the last room. A rumpled bed. This was where Blake had slept. Had her father slept there, too?

She stepped back and crashed into Blake. He cupped her shoulders to steady her. Embarrassment filled every pore, and she pushed past him, heading for fresh air.

Blake followed her outside. "What're you so upset about?"

Arggh. How could he be so dense? "Nothing."

"I saw—" He waved toward the far room where she'd let herself react to the surroundings.

"It was a long trip. I'm tired."

"Right. I'll just get the rest of my stuff." He headed for the bedroom.

She lowered her shoulders. This wasn't going to be easy. But then why should she be surprised? Nothing to do with her father had ever been easy. She followed Blake and prayed for wisdom to deal with him. "Blake, I want to meet Amy. As soon as possible." She'd been shut out of her sister's life far too long. Well, no more.

He halted, his back to her. "Don't you think you should give me a chance to prepare her?"

Although she didn't care for his harsh tone, she saw the sense in what he said. "Fine. But when?"

She refused to allow him to use it as a delaying technique. She suspected he might try to delay it forever.

"As soon as I get a chance."

Ha. She recognized *that* as a deliberate attempt to delay. "Today then?"

He shrugged and concentrated on pulling things off the desk and dropping them into his bag.

"So I can meet her tonight?"

He turned slowly, his expression fierce. "First let's see how she reacts."

She gave him a hard look. This all had a familiar feel to it. Empty promises. Having her feelings shoved aside by a man's excuses. *Well, not this time, buddy.* She wouldn't allow it. "I will not wait forever."

They did silent battle with their eyes, and then he strode from the room.

She grabbed an empty plastic bag off the counter and headed for the bathroom to collect Blake's stuff and help him on his way. In the medicine cupboard she found a collection of men's cologne and aftershave and began to clean the shelves. One bottle looked weirdly familiar. Red, with a white sailing ship. She smelled the bottle. Why did it send little shivers across her shoulders? The sounds of laughter through her thoughts? A distant memory of a little girl on a swing, arcing skyward, giggling? Her throat tightened. How odd.

"You found Rob's Old Spice."

Blake's voice behind her startled her, and she dropped the bottle. It broke, and the scent almost choked her.

"I'll get a rag."

She was still staring at the mess at her feet when he returned with paper towels and swiped up the mess.

"Sorry," she mumbled, backing out of the room.

"You'll be stuck with the smell."

She coughed. Why was she letting a little bottle of outdated aftershave upset her equilibrium? A truly stupid reaction. She swung her gaze to the outdoors. "There's lots of fresh air."

He dropped the paper towels and broken glass into a bag and tied it shut. "I'll get rid of this." He tossed it in the back of his truck, then returned for the box. "I'm out of here."

She couldn't blame him for the bitter note in his voice. After all, this house meant a lot to him. To her, it was more like a guilt offering. One she didn't want and wouldn't accept. Only one thing made her stay. Amy. "I'll expect to see my sister very soon."

He didn't even glance back as he climbed into his truck and drove out of the yard.

❧

Blake drove away from the old house and its memories, his frustration burning like a spray of battery acid. Why had Rob involved his older daughter? Now he was stuck with a woman who would march into his life—and Amy's—then leave. If her past were any indication, the visit would never be repeated. In the meantime, he had to pretend to be nice. And everything in him rebelled at the idea.

He remembered the passage they'd been discussing at Bible study. Something to the effect of forgiving those who have sinned against you. He couldn't remember the exact wording because at the time he didn't see how it applied to him. He didn't hold grudges. Didn't need to forgive anyone.

He gripped the steering wheel, arms and shoulders tight with frustration. And wasn't that just the point? Darcy hadn't hurt him—she'd hurt Rob. And now he carried a grudge on behalf of his stepfather. For years after Rob moved to the ranch, there was no contact between Darcy and Rob. Blake wondered about it occasionally, but they were all busy and content. Except for the picture on the bookshelf, Rob seemed to have erased his previous life from his thoughts. Blake accepted the situation with a certain amount of gratitude. Perhaps a little self-righteous pride that Rob seemed to prefer his present circumstances over anything from the past.

And then suddenly, out of the blue, Darcy had sent Rob an invitation to her high school graduation. His mom was included. Rob had been cautiously happy about it. Mom kept saying it was the beginning of reconciliation. Rob could face his past and deal with it instead of ignoring it. Rob always answered by kissing Blake's mom and saying he preferred to enjoy what he'd found here.

Blake pressed his lips together and let the pain pass.

But the visit never happened. Mom ended up in the hospital. Her unexpected pregnancy with Amy revealed her weak heart. She tried to persuade Rob to go alone, assuring him she'd be well taken care of in the hospital, but Rob refused to leave her side. He called to explain, but Darcy never gave him a chance. She said she never wanted to hear from him again. Rob shrugged and said perhaps it was best to leave things as they were.

Blake couldn't agree more. He'd attempted to talk Rob out of trying to find Darcy when he got sick. Just a few days before he died, Rob expressed regret that he'd failed. Blake's jaw clenched. He had to prevent Amy from going through the same disappointment Rob had with Darcy. He pulled up to the barn and hoisted the bag of cat food to his shoulder. The supply room door swung open, Amy riding it, her toes jammed against the board on the bottom.

"Did you get the food?" she called.

He studied this little sister who meant the world to him. Dirt smudged her cheeks. Cat hair clung to her ragged jeans. He guessed she'd been out here playing with her pets since he left. He tried not to see the likeness between the sisters. "Cat food and a present from your boyfriend."

She gave him a disdainful look, her lips pursed like a big kiss. "I don't have a boyfriend."

"Then I guess you don't want this sucker Joe sent you?" He held up the red candy.

"Oh, Joe. He's not a boyfriend. He's old. Maybe as old as you." She reached for the sucker, yanked the paper off, and popped the candy into her mouth.

"Joe said to say hi." Blake shook his head and pretended to be puzzled. "He seems to think a lot of you. Sure you won't break his heart by saying he's not your boyfriend?"

She shrugged. "Maybe when I'm older."

He chuckled as he set the cat food in the corner.

She dropped off the door and followed him. "Whatcha going to do now?"

"I've got some cows and calves to look after."

"Can I come?"

"Not this time, pumpkin." One of the cows was unpredictable. No place for a little girl.

"Aw." The kid could pack a whole world of emotion into that little sound. "I got nothing to do."

"Why don't you go up to the house and put together one of your jigsaw puzzles?"

Amy drooped her shoulders and hung her head in a way that would win her an Oscar if she were playing a kid in one of London's eighteenth-century orphanages. "Already did my puzzles today."

"Then play with your stuffed animals."

She sighed long and loud. "Don't want to."

"It's almost suppertime. Maybe you should go clean up."

She ignored his suggestion.

"Come on—get on my back, and I'll give you a ride to the house." He had to change his boots before he headed into the corrals.

She climbed the fence and jumped on his back. He trotted to the house, bouncing her until she giggled. "I have to go to the bathroom."

He jerked to a halt. "Not on my back." But when he tried to shake her off, she clung like a stubborn cowboy set on winning the day's purse at a rodeo.

He leaned over his knees, pretending to be exhausted. "Okay, you win, but don't have an accident on me."

She giggled. A sound that made him grin. He felt like a superhero to be the one who made her forget to be sad for a minute. They'd both lost so much; yet they could still enjoy each other.

He continued his journey toward the house, his steps slow and measured. Where was Darcy when Amy had been born? Where was she when Amy and Blake's mother died and Rob was too grief stricken to deal with Amy? The task had fallen on Blake. And where was Darcy when Rob got sick and Blake became more and more responsible for Amy? Why had Rob involved Darcy in Amy's care? He had trusted Rob since before the man married Blake's mom. Yet he had to wonder at this decision.

At the house he dropped Amy to the ground and shooed her upstairs to change her clothes. "Wouldn't hurt you to have a bath either."

Amy shrugged. Blake promised himself to supervise bath time tonight.

He changed his boots and headed out to tackle his work. He sighed wearily and rubbed at his neck. No way he'd finish everything today, which meant that much more to do tomorrow. He was beginning to think he'd never catch up. And now one more thing to deal with. Darcy Hagen and her joint guardianship of Amy.

He'd keep her from seeing Amy if he thought he could, but all he could realistically hope to do was delay it as long as possible. Maybe Darcy would get tired of hanging around and take herself off on her planned vacation.

Except she'd made it plain that wasn't going to happen, and if she were anywhere near as stubborn as Amy. . .

Well, he knew she wouldn't leave until she got what she

wanted. About all he could do was try to protect Amy from being hurt because it seemed Darcy didn't get it—Amy had been through more than her share of loss in her six years. She didn't need a sister who blew into her life and out again.

He suddenly remembered his mother. After his father died, Blake had struggled with anger and resentment. Looking back, he understood there was a lot of fear as to how they would cope. Even then, at twelve, he saw his mother's pain. But she remained serene and confident, explaining they had a choice—wallow in their sorrow and fret about the what-ifs—or trust God. She had quoted a passage in Isaiah so often the words were blazed in his memory.

> *"But now, this is what the Lord says—he who created you, O Jacob, he who formed you, O Israel: 'Fear not, for I have redeemed you; I have summoned you by name; you are mine. When you pass through the waters, I will be with you; and when you pass through the rivers, they will not sweep over you. When you walk through the fire, you will not be burned; the flames will not set you ablaze. For I am the Lord, your God, the Holy One of Israel, your Savior.'"*

He didn't know if Darcy was a river threatening to drown him or a fire waiting to burn him, but who and what she was didn't change God's care and protection. He would follow his mother's advice and choose to trust God in this.

Which meant he had to prepare Amy to meet her sister.

three

Darcy scrubbed the floor vehemently—a wonderful catharsis for her anger and frustration. She'd waited hours last night for Blake to bring Amy over. She'd practically glued herself to the doorframe, looking toward the two-story house across the yard. A nice comfortable distance for country neighbors, she guessed. Close enough to be able to see a person walking around outside, yet far enough you couldn't see in the windows.

She'd memorized her view of the house. White siding, green shingles, three sets of windows facing her on the upstairs. Downstairs, four big windows on one side of the wide front doors and three smaller ones on the other side. She guessed most of the traffic went in and out of the back of the house, toward the barns and fences. And where she couldn't see.

She'd stared at the house for hours, waiting for Blake to appear with a girl at his side. She tried to picture the girl. Would she come up to Blake's shoulder, or was she still knee-high?

But Blake failed to show. Finally, as darkness closed in around her, she gave up, changed into an old, familiar pair of jeans, and turned her energies toward scrubbing the house until it squeaked a protest. She worked late into the night and again this morning, all the time fuming.

Blake might have bought himself a few more hours, but that was all. Only concern for her little sister kept her from marching up to the other house and demanding entrance. In all fairness someone should prepare Amy. But if Blake didn't, Darcy would. She just had to figure out the best way.

She prayed for wisdom as she scoured the dirt off every shelf, cleaned every cupboard, and polished the windowpanes.

She finished washing the floor, sat back on her heels to admire her job, and grimaced at her red, wrinkled hands. She'd have to slather on lotion and give herself a manicure tonight, but it was worth it to see *her* house cleaned. Despite her anger and frustration over Blake not doing what she expected, as she scrubbed she experienced the foreign emotion of belonging. For every speck of dust she captured, every smudge she removed, every retreating bit of dirt she swept up, her joy grew. She *owned* this house, unlike every other landlord-owned, temporary home she'd known. She never guessed having her name on a title would make such a difference. She snorted, mocking her fanciful thoughts. Of course, she'd sell it and return to Seattle. But it was hers. Hers to keep or sell.

"What're you doing in Blake's house?"

The clear sound of a child's voice jerked Darcy's attention to the door where a small face pressed against the screen, lips bubbled into graph-paper squares.

Darcy's heart knocked at her chest as wave after wave of emotion swept through her. Surprise. Regret. Disbelief. And a hundred things she couldn't identify. She couldn't breathe. It was like the air had been vacuumed from the room. She couldn't move. She couldn't hear or smell or think. An intense feeling of loss crashed over her. Tears stung her eyes.

She stared at the little girl. Blond hair tangled around her head like a bad case of bed head. Blue eyes wide, she regarded Darcy with a familiar expression. She might have been looking at a picture of herself as a child. Except this girl had blond hair.

Slowly she rose, setting the pail of dirty water in the sink.

"This is Blake's house," the girl said, her tone challenging.

"Didn't Blake tell you about me?"

The girl shook her head.

Humph. How like a man to promise to do something and then not do it. "Do you want to come in?"

She hesitated, then jerked the door open and slipped in to stand just inside the room, her expression cautious.

Darcy took a step closer, but as the child's shoulders tensed she stopped and studied the tiny girl in front of her. She wore dirty jeans, torn at the knees and frayed at the bottom, and a T-shirt too wide at the bottom and sagging at the neck.

"You're Amy, aren't you?" Her words caught in her tight throat.

Amy nodded. "Who are you?"

Darcy smiled at the way Amy hid her fear behind a demanding tone. "I'm Darcy. How old are you?"

"Six. Whatcha doing in Blake's house?"

"I'm cleaning it." And scrambling mentally to figure out what to tell her. Should she confess she was an older sister? And then how to explain why Amy had never seen her before? Or even heard of her. And what did she say about the guardianship issue? Would you tell a child this small such things? She didn't have a clue. About all she could remember about being that size was her disappointment when her daddy left. If only he had explained it to her, made sure she didn't blame herself. Ah. So she'd answered her own questions. Even a tiny child deserved honesty.

"How come? Is Blake going to live here now?" Darcy heard the tremor of fear in Amy's voice that even her belligerence didn't disguise.

"No. I am."

"You can't. It's Blake's. You can't change things."

"Doesn't Blake live with you?"

Amy nodded.

"You wouldn't want to change that, would you?"

"No." Amy crossed her arms over her chest and stuck out her chin as if daring anyone to try.

"Then he doesn't need this house anymore."

"Didja buy it?"

"Not exactly."

"Then you can't have it."

Darcy laughed. She loved the stubborn streak she glimpsed in her little sister. One thing she admired was someone who stuck to her beliefs. "Someone gave it to me."

"Who? Blake?"

"No. Your father."

For just a moment Amy's expression crumpled; then she widened her eyes. "My daddy's gone to heaven."

Darcy squatted to eye level and touched Amy's shoulder. "I know. I'm sorry. You must miss him a lot."

Tears washed Amy's eyes as she nodded. "My mommy and daddy both went to heaven so they could be together."

"Ah, sweetie. I'm so sorry." She opened her arms. Amy hesitated a moment, then threw herself against Darcy. Darcy staggered back under her assault and landed on her bottom. She sat on the floor holding the crying child.

After a minute the tears stopped, but Amy remained with her face cradled against Darcy's neck.

"How come he gave you the house?" Amy's breath was warm.

Darcy held back her anger at Blake for putting her in this position and tried to think how and what she should tell Amy. About all she could do was answer her questions as honestly as possible. If Blake didn't approve, he should have taken care of it himself. But she didn't know Amy and didn't know how she'd react. She silently prayed for wisdom. She inhaled slowly, then spoke softly. "Because he was my daddy, too."

Amy leaned back and stared into Darcy's face, her eyes narrowed in concentration. "He wasn't Blake's daddy."

"I know."

"Then how come he's your daddy?"

"He was my daddy before he married your mommy."

"Is Blake your brother?"

"No." She explained as simply as possible how she could be Amy's sister, yet not be Blake's sister.

Amy settled back on her heels and looked Darcy up and down. Twice. She squinted into Darcy's eyes.

Darcy hardly dared breathe as she let Amy study her. She knew from Amy's look of concentration that she was assessing the information she'd just received. Darcy wondered what her reaction would be.

"Were you his little girl?" Amy asked.

The words clawed at Darcy. She pressed her hand to her chest to ease the pain. "Once upon a time I was."

"You look like the little girl in the picture."

"What picture is that?"

Amy shrugged. "Just a little girl in a picture." Her eyes misted with sadness. "My daddy's gone forever."

Darcy pulled Amy toward her. "I know how much you miss him." She remembered the feeling well. Waiting day after day, desperately hoping. Endlessly wanting. Until she'd made the decision to stop torturing herself. At least Amy would be spared the uncertainty and continual disappointment. Her parting was complete and explainable.

"But you know he's in heaven now." Darcy couldn't go on. Had her father become a Christian? He wasn't when she knew him. Her mother had only become one a few years ago.

Amy nodded. "He's with my mommy. He promised me I would see him when I go to heaven."

"That's good then, isn't it?"

"I miss my daddy so much." Amy started to cry. "But I don't want to die."

"Oh, honey." She hugged Amy fiercely, her heart bleeding at Amy's pain. "I'm certain your daddy doesn't mind waiting. He knows you have so many things to discover yet and so much stuff to do. The world is just waiting for Amy Hagen to do the things only Amy can do."

Amy leaned back. "Really?"

"Of course. That's why God made you. So you could do the Amy things in the world."

"Like what?"

Please, Lord. Give me the right words. She thought of when she'd started going to church. "I remember when my mom and I moved to a new house. I was about thirteen. There was a nice lady living next door, Mrs. Roland, and she invited me to go to church with her. She taught a class of girls my age and encouraged us to learn Bible verses we could use as guidelines for life. She gave us really neat rewards if we learned all the ones she chose." Even though Amy listened closely, Darcy was sure she didn't want to hear about the sleepovers and camping trips Mrs. R took them on. Nor that it was through Mrs. R's love and gentleness that Darcy found her way to God. "I think some of those verses might help you see what I mean. 'Whatever your hand finds to do, do it with all your might.' 'Rejoice before the Lord your God in everything you put your hand to.'"

She smiled into the eyes that were so much like the ones she saw in the mirror every day. "That means whatever is in front of you to do, that's your job. You should do it well and be happy."

"Like feeding my cats?"

Darcy nodded.

"I like feeding my cats."

"There are Amy jobs everywhere. Going to school, being kind to your friends, giving out free smiles."

Amy giggled, then sobered so suddenly Darcy knew she'd been surprised by a thought. "How come I never heard of you?"

Darcy's throat tightened, and she rocked her head back and forth, and breathed slowly before she could speak. "I don't know."

Amy jerked to her feet. "You're my big sister."

Darcy nodded.

Amy stared openmouthed and then smiled so wide it must have hurt. In fact, Darcy knew it did because her smile matched Amy's.

They grinned into each other's eyes for a full, sweet minute; then Darcy got to her feet. "I have a present for you." Amy followed Darcy as she padded barefoot into the bedroom and retrieved the parcel she'd brought from the store. "It's a welcome-sister present."

Amy tore the bag open and pulled out the catnip balls and bell toys. "For my cats. Goody. They love toys." She looked uncertain. "I don't have a welcome present for you."

"But you do." She was the best present one could ever expect, but Darcy knew that wasn't what Amy meant.

"What?"

"A big hug and kiss."

"Aww. That's nothing."

"It means a lot to me." Darcy sat on the edge of the bed and opened her arms. Amy planted a warm, generous kiss on her cheek and hugged her so tight Darcy almost choked.

❧

Blake finished the barn chores and headed straight for the house. He'd planned to sit down with Amy last night and tell her about Darcy, but the yearling steers had broken down the fence and gotten in with the cows and calves. It was a mess and totally preventable. He'd noticed the loose planks on the fence days ago but kept running out of daylight before he could fix it. In the long run it would have saved him time to get to it somehow.

It had taken him three hot and frustrating hours to fix the fence, then separate out the steers and put them back in their own pen.

And then the maternity pen demanded attention.

By the time he'd cleaned it all up and headed for the house, it was long past Amy's bedtime. Aunt Betty had bathed her and put her to bed, and then had gone to bed herself.

Aunt Betty, bless her heart, had left food out for him. She wasn't the world's best cook. She favored macaroni cooked to the consistency of glue, colored with processed cheese. Sometimes she varied her menus with scrambled eggs, fried hamburger, and canned vegetables, but she seldom bothered with the grade-A steaks and roasts in the freezer. To make up for Aunt Betty's lack of culinary skills, Blake kept the fridge stocked with fresh fruit and other healthy treats for Amy to snack on. Their diet was adequate despite his craving for a good meat-and-potatoes meal.

The cold food Aunt Betty left held no appeal. He scraped what remained into the garbage and built a thick peanut butter-jelly sandwich. The nutrition-deprived white bread stuck to the roof of his mouth as he chowed down on it. He could vaguely remember thick slices of homemade bread, nutty rich with freshly ground whole-wheat flour. His mother had made the best bread in the world before she got too weak to do anything but care for Amy. He chased the sandwich with a tall glass of milk, rubbed a weary hand over his aching eyes, and thanked God for the temporary reprieve in dealing with the elder Hagen daughter.

But things were under control this morning—for a few hours—and he hurried to the house to find Amy. He'd tried to decide how to tell her about Darcy. But how did he explain why she'd suddenly shown up? Why she'd never contacted any of them? It was due to her own neglect she didn't know about Amy, but he had no idea how to put a positive spin on it for his little sister.

"Aunt Betty, where's Amy?"

The woman was mixing up the special diet she prepared for her old, ailing cat named Missy. The cat had seen better days and elicited more affection and attention from Aunt

Betty than he understood. He was, nevertheless, grateful for the older woman's help. Her idiosyncrasies seemed minor in comparison to what some of the other nannies had inflicted on him. He'd endured everything from hot pursuit to huge long-distance charges on his telephone.

Aunt Betty paused a moment to answer him. "She was playing next to the house."

"I'll see what she's up to." Amy wasn't next to the house. He checked upstairs, but she wasn't among the scattered stuffed animals or on the rumpled bed. He picked her dirty sneakers off the pillow and carried them down to the back entryway where he dropped them on the floor. "I'll have another look in the barn."

He searched the supply room and wandered through the machine shed, calling her name. Nothing. She wasn't on the swing set in the backyard. She wasn't under the tree where she often played. He stood in the middle of the yard, rubbing his chin. Where had she disappeared to this time? His gaze shifted to the low house half hidden in the trees not more than five hundred yards away.

It wouldn't have taken more than a few minutes for her to discover the unfamiliar car parked over there, and knowing her curiosity. . .

His neck went into full-out spasm. What was he thinking not to tell her about Darcy before this? As he jogged toward the house, he uttered a desperate prayer he would get there before Amy made any unpleasant discoveries. Why had Rob brought this on them? What was God thinking to allow it?

He headed for the back door. His boots echoed across the wooden deck. He caught a whiff of something that made his taste buds spring to life with a vengeance. Then he heard Amy laughing and skidded to a halt. Battered by so many losses, Amy never laughed with anyone but him. Not since Rob's death. Hot protectiveness scorched up his throat. He would not let his fragile little sister be hurt by this woman.

Through the screen door he heard Amy's voice. "Do I put them in now?" she asked.

"Yes. And now you have to stir it." A pause. "Gently."

Blake smiled. Amy didn't do anything gently. He knocked.

"It's open!" Darcy called.

Blake stepped into the kitchen and stared. The two of them stood before the stove, Amy on a chair as she stirred a pot. The similarity between the two was unmistakable. Both wore old jeans and baggy T-shirts. They smiled at each other with the same pleasure-filled expression. The same wide blue eyes. Due to the difference in their ages, the sisters looked like mother and daughter.

Memories fired across his brain. When his mother was alive, he'd lived with scenes like this—domestic scenes full of food and love and warmth. Mom flipping pancakes. Her pride in her homemade spaghetti sauce. The special smile she reserved for him. He always felt so warm and welcomed in her presence. Would he ever know that homey feeling again? Did Amy remember standing on a stool next to their mother, chattering away like a bird?

An ache as wide as the blue Montana sky swallowed up his insides. The what-ifs and if-onlys that haunted him late at night when he couldn't sleep rushed forward for attention, but only in the depths of the darkness did he admit he longed for a home such as he'd known. A woman who smiled at him and greeted him as if her world revolved around him. Instead he had Aunt Betty and the responsibility of his precious little sister.

He pushed aside the memories, shoved the pain into hiding. He had Amy to take care of now. He wouldn't let anything—anyone—hurt her. He had neither room nor time for more. The hole in his life would never be filled.

He focused on Amy. She looked different. It took a moment

for him to realize her hair had been brushed back into a ponytail matching Darcy's hairdo.

The delicious aromas made Blake's stomach growl.

"Amy," he said. "You shouldn't be here."

Two pairs of blue eyes looked at him with scorn.

"Why not?" Amy demanded.

Even though Darcy didn't speak, he read her silent echo of the words. "Aunt Betty's worried about you."

"Why?" Amy's question was blunt. "I can look after myself."

Both pairs of eyes turned back toward the bubbling pot from which came aromas of tomato and garlic. The smell was enough to drive a man mad.

"We're making chicken ziti," Amy said. "Right, Darcy?"

"That's right." Darcy flicked a glance toward Blake. "There's plenty. You're welcome to stay for lunch." She looked at Amy as she spoke, her gaze filled with such hunger Blake immediately forgot his appetite.

"Can we, please, Blake? Please?" Amy would have bounced off the chair if Darcy hadn't caught her.

When the two sisters looked at each other and giggled, Blake's insides filled with fire. He didn't want Amy to be hurt. "Aunt Betty will expect us. We have to go."

Amy pushed her bottom lip out so far he could have hung his hat on it. "I don't like what Aunt Betty cooks." She made a gagging sound.

Blake's stomach threatened to revolt at the thought of choking down another meal of unappetizing food. But staying here was not an option. "The food is perfectly adequate."

Darcy lifted Amy down. "You'd better go home. Thanks for your help."

Amy hugged Darcy. "I want to stay here."

Darcy hugged her back and laughed. "You just want to eat my food." But Blake saw the sheen of tears.

"Run along, pumpkin," he told Amy. "I'll be right there."

Amy slammed out of the door.

Blake waited until he heard her footsteps pounding away before he faced Darcy. "She shouldn't have been here."

Darcy gave him the same defiant stare Amy had. Great. This was going to be fun, dealing with two of them.

"Why not? She's my sister, and I have, need I remind you, joint guardianship of her."

"I can't imagine what Rob was thinking when he did that."

"Me either. Unless it was guilt."

"Guilt for what?"

"You'd never understand."

"Listen to me. Amy is going through a difficult time, and I don't want anything to make it worse. Besides, she didn't have permission to come here. I've been looking all over for her."

"So tell her to ask permission before she comes back."

"You just don't get it, do you? I don't want her visiting here."

Darcy succeeded in looking as if he'd slapped her. "No, *you* don't get it." She jerked her gaze away, turned the burners off, and wiped her hands on a towel. "I think we need to talk." Her eyes were as hard as her tone. "Why don't we sit at the table?"

He hesitated. He didn't want to spend any more time in this house than he had to. It was too full of memories—memories he couldn't afford to think about. He had far too many responsibilities to linger on the past. But she was right. They needed to settle this. The sooner the better. Then she could return to her vacation schedule, and he could get on with his work.

He crossed the floor and parked himself on the chair next to the patio doors.

"Coffee?" She began to pour a cup.

"No, thanks." He regretted his answer as she poured the coffee down the drain and sat across from him.

She studied her hands clasped in her lap, then slowly brought her gaze upward. Her generous smile caught him off guard. Maybe he'd misjudged her.

"You said you would tell Amy about me."

He shrugged. "Something came up."

As did her eyebrows at his excuse. "I see. No, actually, I don't. But it doesn't matter. I told her we were sisters."

He couldn't get rid of the churning, burning bile taste in his stomach. He had prayed for strength to deal with this. He was intent on trusting God. But all he had to do was sit across the table from her, look into her determined face, and his good resolutions fled like snow in a heat wave.

"I've left it to you to tell Amy about the guardianship order." She made it sound as if she'd done him a favor.

"I don't mean to tell her." Now when had he decided that? Why did this woman make him put his brain in park and drive with his errant emotions? He gave himself a mental shake. Nothing about this woman could be allowed to distract him from what really mattered—protecting Amy.

She stared at him. "Why not? Kids deserve the truth."

"What would be the point? Don't you see how stupid and useless it would be? You're leaving again in"—he glanced at his watch, hoping she would get the none-too-subtle hint that he hoped it would be very soon—"how long, did you say?"

"I didn't."

"What's to keep you here?" No need to remind her she wasn't interested in visiting when her father was alive. When she might have had a reason.

"Amy."

He planted his fists on the table as he leaned toward her. "What are you trying to do? Mess her up? She's had enough to deal with. She doesn't need a sister"—he sneered the word—"who is here today, gone tomorrow. Just leave her alone." He leaned back. "Leave us all alone."

She looked hurt and confused. *Nice touch*, he thought. *Try to make me feel sympathetic. But it's not going to work.* He relaxed as stubbornness set into her features. This emotion he understood.

"I want to get to know her better."

"Don't mess with her. She's just a kid."

"I'm not going to hurt her, if that's what concerns you. I know what it's like to be a kid and be disappointed by adults you care about."

The skin around his eyes tightened. "You keep suggesting you were a poor, helpless victim of some injustice. Sorry. I don't buy it. And I won't let you blame Rob, especially when he's not here to defend himself. You could have visited him anytime you wanted, but you didn't. How am I supposed to think you won't treat Amy the same way?" He pushed back from the table and stood over her. "Don't you think it would be best for everyone concerned if you let the lawyer look after arranging the sale of this house so you can get on with your vacation?"

She grabbed his wrist before he could escape. "Wait." An electric shock raced up his nerves at her cool touch. "I've decided to stay for a few days, so can't we be civil about this?"

He jerked away. "There is no room in my life for anything but my work and Amy. So if you're going to stay, I suggest you keep out of my way."

She huffed. "Like that's going to be a problem. But what about Amy?"

"What about her?"

"Is she going to be allowed to visit me?"

He glowered at her, matching her look for look. "Are you the least bit concerned with what's best for her?"

Again he caught a fleeting look of pain that made him feel like a heartless bully. Then she lifted her chin, and he wondered if he'd imagined it.

"Yes, I am. I see a little girl who's hurting from the death of her parents. I think I can help her." She didn't blink under his stare.

He felt himself dragged into the significance of what she said. As if she knew how to deal with loss. As if she knew the shape of pain. He stared out the window. If she did she had no one to blame but herself, and he was getting thoroughly sick of her suggesting it was Rob's fault. No disrespect to his own father, but Rob had been the best father a man could ask for.

"Unless you're afraid." Her soft voice rang with challenge.

"What would I be afraid of?"

She lifted one shoulder. "Are you sure it's Amy you're trying to protect? Or yourself? Maybe you can't handle the possibility she might find someone besides you to care about."

Anger stomped through him, indignant and hot. How dare she assign her motives to him? But he'd let her accusation go unchallenged if it gained him an advantage. And he knew exactly what he hoped to gain by ignoring her words. "I'll let Amy visit on one condition."

"Name it."

"When you leave you give up your guardianship."

She stepped back. "You can't be serious."

He had her cornered. "Aren't we talking about what's best for Amy?" He kept his voice soft, pressing his advantage. "You live in Seattle. How can you begin to think you could have input into her daily life?"

She turned her back to him, stirred the savory-smelling concoction. "You're right, of course." Her words were soft. "But I'm afraid I can't agree to your one condition." She swung around to face him, her expression fierce. "I will not lose my little sister. Not when I've just found her. And I won't let you keep us from enjoying each other."

He blinked and tried not to admire her guts in challenging

him, even as anger chewed through his insides at her failure to agree to his very good plan. He closed his eyes for a moment and prayed for patience. Tons of it. Immediately.

"You have two weeks off?"

She nodded.

In two weeks she'd be gone and out of their lives. And if her past was any indication, they'd probably never hear from her again.

She suddenly grinned. "Do you realize I might be doing you a favor?"

He snorted. "How's that?"

"She's on spring break, right?" She barely waited for his nod. "Seems she could use a little more supervision." He started to protest even though he knew it was true. He just didn't need an outsider coming in and pointing it out. But she went on steadily, not giving him a chance to pull his thoughts into a coherent argument. "I can help keep her entertained." She shrugged as if to suggest the advantages were obvious. And even though he didn't want to agree, he knew she was right.

They stared at each other. He wouldn't blink first. Finally she smiled, a conciliatory gesture. Her eyes turned sunny blue. She was nothing like he'd expected. And it wasn't just her resemblance to Amy. It was the quickening of emotions that danced through her eyes before she could hide it. She seemed almost normally human with regular emotions, which he wouldn't have thought possible twenty-four hours ago. Something inside him yielded. He put it down to God showing him it was okay to give in on this.

"Two weeks, and then you'll be gone." It was more of an order than a question. Her smile fled, and he instantly regretted his harshness.

"I have to return to my job."

"I'll tell Aunt Betty that Amy has permission to come whenever she wants."

Darcy's eyes brightened. "Thank you."

He snickered. "You might not be thanking me in a few days, after you've had Amy barging in here like a runaway freight train whenever she feels like it."

Darcy shook her head, smiling widely. "You're wrong. I'll still be thanking you."

He wondered if her voice trembled just a tiny bit.

four

Darcy pressed her arms across her stomach and stared out the window until she could no longer hear Blake's receding footsteps. Only then did she let the intermingling waves of pain, shock, rage, and grief wash over her. It was tempting to cry. To scream and rail against *her* loss.

She pulled herself together. She'd forgiven the past, her father's abandonment. She'd learned to lean on God as her strength and healer. But right now she couldn't seem to separate her faith from her feelings.

She hurried to the bedroom, pulled her cell phone from her purse, and punched in a familiar number. It rang twice before someone answered.

"Mrs. R. I'm so glad you're home. I hope I'm not bothering you. I need to talk to someone," she wailed.

The older woman chuckled. "You are never a bother."

Darcy smiled. Mrs. R always said the same thing, and Darcy always liked to hear it.

"How are you?" Mrs. R asked. "Or should I ask, where are you?"

"At the ranch where my father lived." She explained the events of the past day to her longtime friend and mentor, imagining her sitting in her big armchair, her salt-and-pepper hair in a wild disarray of curls, her Bible next to her, a notebook open on her lap as she made notes for her Sunday school class. Her gray eyes always so watchful and kind, as if every word Darcy uttered, even as an eager new Christian, mattered more than the next breath.

"Sounds like God has a purpose for your visit beyond the

reading of a will."

"You mean Amy, don't you?" Darcy sighed. "She's a sweetie, for sure. And hurting."

"I don't just mean Amy, though I'm sure you'll be a real comfort to her. I mean you, dear. This can be a time of healing for you."

Darcy gripped the phone so hard it beeped a protest. "I thought I'd dealt with all this stuff about my father." At first she hated him and resented the new family, but it was a destructive emotion. Through Mrs. R's counseling and pointing Darcy toward God's love, she'd let all that go. "But being here and listening to Blake tell what a wonderful father he was—" She couldn't go on as pain pierced her soul.

"Forgiveness is a choice; healing takes time."

Darcy rocked back and forth. "I don't want to go back to all that stuff. I just want to move forward."

"That stuff, as you call it, will always be part of who you are, how you feel and react."

"You know what really hurts?"

"What, dear?"

"Blake thinks I should stay away from Amy." She repeated Blake's ultimatum. As she talked, she wandered into the kitchen and faced the slanting rays of the sun coming through the sunporch. "Amy and I clicked. To think I missed six years of her life. I will never forg—" She made herself stop as she realized the mistake of what she'd been about to say. Of course she forgave everyone concerned. She had long ago learned the futility of anything less. "I've missed enough of her life. I intend to enjoy every minute of my vacation with her."

"What happens when you have to go back to work?" Mrs. R asked softly.

Ahh. Something twisted in Darcy's gut as her friend's words echoed Blake's concern. "I guess we'll make some sort of arrangement." Perhaps both Blake and Mrs. R were right.

Maybe she should move on now. After all, they didn't need her. They had each other. She had her life. But telling herself so didn't change how she felt. She wanted to be part of Amy's life. She needed to feel she mattered to Amy.

"I'll be praying for you to have wisdom and strength to deal with this situation." Mrs. R's words smoothed Darcy's emotions.

"Thank you. I don't know what will happen. I just know I won't walk away. I've been deprived of my little sister too long."

"And she's been deprived of you."

"Yes." Mrs. R made it sound like an equal loss.

"I suppose you're right." Despite Blake's objections, Darcy knew there was something important about being a big sister. "I'll do my best for her while I'm here, and then we'll decide where to go from there." She took a deep breath. "Thanks as always, Mrs. R."

The older woman laughed. "When are you going to start calling me Olive?"

Darcy laughed, too. It was a long-standing joke between them. "When I'm older than you." She paused. "You know I like calling you Mrs. R."

The woman laughed. "You just like making me aware of my age."

Darcy chuckled. "You haven't aged a year in all the time I've known you. Nope, I just like you being Mrs. R, the woman who saw past my anger as a teenager and loved me into God's family."

"You were easy to love. Still are."

"Thank you." She hung up a few minutes later, feeling refreshed. She knew why she was here. Because of Amy. Not even Blake's resistance would make her leave.

She dragged a chair out to the sunroom and called Irene to bring her up to speed.

"He sounds like a nice man," Irene said after Darcy finished telling her all the news.

"Probably is, except he doesn't like me. In fact, he's made it clear he'd like nothing better than for me to leave ASAP. Or sooner."

"Want me to come out and persuade him otherwise?"

Darcy imagined Irene flexing her arms and laughed. "I'll call you if I need some muscle."

"Promise? He sounds like my sort of man."

Darcy made a choking noise.

"Don't say it," Irene warned.

Darcy took a deep breath and tried to sound bewildered. "What is it I'm not supposed to say?"

Irene sighed dramatically. "That I never met a man I didn't like."

They laughed together and chatted a few minutes longer. Darcy felt tons better after talking to two of her closest friends. With God's help she would find the grace to deal with this situation.

⁂

Blake didn't go directly to the house. He was too upset to risk meeting Amy or Aunt Betty. Instead he went to the shop and began repairing the cultivator. Bad enough he was stuck with Darcy for two weeks. Now he had to sit back and let his little sister spend as much time as she wanted with the woman. How was Amy supposed to deal with all this? But his loyalty to Rob caused him the most confusion. He'd loved the man. He'd also trusted Rob totally and completely. A niggling doubt skidded over his thoughts. Until now. Yet, knowing Rob, he knew the man must have had a reason for bringing Darcy into their lives. Something more than the misguided guilt Darcy suggested.

He heard a shuffling sound and turned to see Amy in the doorway, her face folded into a scowl. He could no longer put off talking to her about Darcy. He leaned the hammer against the cupboard and wiped his hands on a rag. "Let's go see your cats."

She followed him without a word, although her mutinous expression spoke volumes. She was going to have some hard questions for him.

At the supply room he waited while Amy filled the cat dishes and murmured to the animals. He wasn't surprised to be excluded from her conversation.

When he and Amy were both sprawled comfortably on the floor, he asked, "What did Darcy tell you?"

She crossed her arms and plunked them over her chest. "She's my sister."

"Uh-huh."

"The house is hers."

"That's right."

She scooted away several inches. Blake told himself it was only Amy showing her displeasure, but the little gesture made it clear that no matter what Darcy did or said, it was going to affect the rest of them.

"How come you never told me about her?"

"There didn't seem to be any point. I never expected she'd ever come. She's never been here before."

"How come?"

"I really can't say." Though he had his own opinions. Too self-centered. Full of bitter unforgiveness. Jealous. Any or all of the above.

"How come Daddy didn't tell me about her?"

"I don't know." In hindsight he, too, wondered. But then Darcy had never given any of them any reason to include her in their lives.

Amy studied him hard, her expression thoughtful. "Is she your sister?"

"No. She's your half sister. Just like I'm your half brother."

He tried to explain the convoluted relationship but wondered if it made sense to Amy.

She giggled. "You're half a brother."

He growled low in his throat. "I'm all here, thank you very much."

She tipped her head and looked serious. "How come you didn't want to see her before?"

He shrugged. He could hardly tell her his personal opinion of the woman—without natural affection or a normal sense of duty. "Guess I was too busy to think about it."

Amy harrumphed. "I don't think so."

He chuckled. "Like any of us have had time to run out to Seattle to look for her." He didn't expect Amy to understand how swamped he'd been. For years. Even before Rob got sick, his mother needed help. Seems there had been more work than they could catch up with for a long time.

"I would have gone to see her."

He knew Amy thought she was old enough to tackle anything in her path, but the idea of his little sister on her own made him smile.

"I would have," she insisted.

He ruffled her hair. "Good thing you won't have to. She's here for two weeks. You'll get plenty of chances to visit her." He hesitated. He had to prepare Amy for the inevitable. *Lord, give me wisdom. This situation is more than I know how to deal with.* He gave Amy a gentle look. "Just remember it's only a visit. Then she's leaving again. She lives a long ways away. You might not see her again"—he couldn't leave her without a speck of hope—"for a long time."

Amy sat back and stroked several of the cats who'd finished eating and wrapped themselves around her, purring. "Why can't she stay here?"

Already the regrets and shattered dreams. What would it be like after two weeks? He knew it wasn't going to be pretty.

He leaned closer. "Listen to me, Amy. She's only here for a visit and then gone again. Don't start to think she will stay, or you're going to get hurt, and I don't want that."

Amy's eyes clouded. "But why can't she stay? She's my sister."

Blake rubbed the back of his neck. "She can't. She's got a job back in the city. She lives there. That's all." She couldn't live here. She wouldn't. And she'd likely forget Amy as soon as she left. Poor Amy. He was thankful there was no need to mention the guardianship thing. Darcy would probably forget it once she was back in Seattle. He was counting on it.

"Come on. Let's go have lunch." He stood and pulled her to her feet. "Want a horsey ride?"

She nodded soberly and climbed to his back. By the time he bounced her halfway across the yard, she was giggling. And he could breathe easy again.

His stomach rumbled as they went into the house. Aunt Betty's idea of lunch was canned tomato soup and grilled cheese sandwiches made with processed cheese between slices of anemic white bread. Sometimes they got a treat and had vegetable soup. Not that he was complaining. It was a perfectly good combination. But every day? It got a little tiresome. He'd bought other things, suggested a few alternatives, but Aunt Betty said she'd grown up with that menu every day and she saw no reason to change it.

Aunt Betty had the food out. She plopped her cat in the blanket-padded box at her feet.

Amy looked at Blake and rolled her eyes, then scowled at the cat who returned her glare with such a disdainful look that Blake shook his head. Amy and the cat hated each other.

Aunt Betty sat down and nodded at Blake to say grace. He had to pause a moment to feel thankful. After his prayer, he turned to his aunt. "Rob left the other house to his older daughter. She's there now."

Aunt Betty nodded. "Thought I saw someone down there."

"Amy has permission to visit her while she's here."

"I do?" Amy asked around her mouthful of sandwich.

Blake nodded. "As long as you don't make a nuisance of yourself. And remember what I told you. She's leaving in two weeks."

"Oh goody, goody, goody. We are going to have so much fun."

Aunt Betty sighed. "Can't say as I mind. Maybe it'll keep her out of trouble."

Blake wasn't sure Amy wasn't substituting one set of "trouble" for another.

"Amy, I'm going to take the four-wheeler and check the pasture fences this afternoon. Want to come along?" He probably wasn't playing fair. Riding the quad was one of Amy's greatest pleasures.

Amy shook her head.

He plunked his fists on the table and stared. Maybe she hadn't heard him. "You can come with me."

"I know." She stared at him, eyes wide.

"You never turn down a chance to ride with me."

"Can't I stay and see Darcy?"

He thought of saying no, but if he forced her to go with him she'd be miserable the whole time. "Sure. But remember. . ."

"I know." She sighed. "Two weeks."

❧

Blake didn't stay out as long as he'd originally planned. Normally he would have bummed a meal somewhere rather than return for supper. Any one of his neighbors would have welcomed him. Especially Norma Shaw, who'd been trying to get Blake interested in her daughter, Jeannie, since Jeannie came back to teach at the school. He might have been more interested if he wasn't already so busy he hardly had time to scrape the crud off his boots.

But Mrs. Shaw and her lovely daughter would have to wait.

He was worried about Amy, restless at the thought of her being with Darcy all afternoon.

"Amy!" he called as he barreled into the house. "Ame, where are you?"

Aunt Betty came from her room, straight pins between her teeth. She removed them so she could speak. "No need to shout down the house. She's over with her sister." She waved the pins at him. "About time I had some peace so I could get these quilts done. Those children in Romania have nothing." She hurried back to her room and her quilting.

Blake wondered if it wouldn't be more charitable for Aunt Betty to give Amy as much of her time as she gave those nameless orphans she knitted and sewed for and for whom she attended endless meetings. He stood in the middle of the room and tried to decide what to do. He had no excuse to run over to the other house. Besides, he probably wouldn't fool Darcy. She'd know he was checking on her.

He had lots of work to choose from, but used to Amy hanging around demanding attention, he felt restless. It seemed he wasn't indispensable anymore. He reluctantly headed for the office. He was in a bad mood anyway; he might as well pay bills.

The box Blake had brought from the other house sat in the middle of the desk. It seemed like a good enough reason to put off the loathsome job of paying bills, but he'd already put it off far too long. He grabbed the box. Smiling up at him from among the books and his roping trophy was the photo of his mother and Rob. They'd all been so happy back then. He put the box in the closet, picked up the picture, and let the missing fill him. He swallowed hard, his eyes burning. He waited for the hurricane of emotions to pass. He looked around for a place to put the picture, saw the old photo of Darcy that Rob always kept on the shelf by the desk, grabbed it, and shoved it in the bottom drawer—an appropriate spot for it. She had no place on this ranch. He put up the picture of Rob and Mom, smiled at them, and sat down to pay bills, comforted by their presence.

five

Suppertime approached. Blake welcomed the excuse to leave the desk, the bills, and the record keeping, almost as much as he welcomed the legitimate reason to take Amy from Darcy's house.

He stood in the afternoon sunshine and stretched. Spring was his favorite time of year. His fingertips hooked in the front pocket of his jeans, he headed across the yard. He heard them before he saw them, recognized Amy's throaty giggle. Then he heard an echoing giggle, sweet as a bird's song. Why did her voice tickle across his senses like music?

At the outside corner of the sunroom, he came to an abrupt halt.

Amy and Darcy sat cross-legged on a black and red blanket he recognized from the closet of the old house. Darcy looked like a flash of sunlight in a bright yellow T-shirt and matching striped pants that ended at her knees. Both the girls wore dandelion chains, piled on their heads like golden crowns and hanging around their necks like happy Hawaiian greetings.

Amy grasped a handful of yellow flowers and reached for Darcy, trying to brush the dandelion butter on her already-painted face.

Blake leaned against the wall and watched Darcy bat Amy's hands away, each time swiping a yellow streak across Amy's already very yellow cheeks.

Darcy ducked out of Amy's reach, laughing as she tumbled over. Amy rolled into Darcy's arms. She hiccupped and giggled. Darcy echoed her, and they exploded into louder giggles, punctuated firmly by more hiccups. Darcy wiped tears away, smudging the yellow into war paint.

As the sisters rolled around like playful puppies, giggling and hiccupping, he let a deep laugh boom out. *"A cheerful heart is good medicine."* Another of his mother's often-quoted Bible verses. How long since he'd enjoyed a belly laugh?

Darcy sat up, pushed Amy to her side, and met his gaze across the greening yard. Her eyes were as blue as summer skies, bright as the flash of running water in the sun, full of magic and fun and welcome and living. Life shared, blessed with the sharing.

Amy saw him, bounced over, and tackled his knees. He grunted and steadied himself without breaking eye contact with Darcy.

"Come play with us!" Amy demanded.

"What are you playing?" He couldn't pull his gaze from Darcy. He didn't want to. His heart bundled up inside his chest and demanded more. He wanted to discover the secret behind her flashing eyes.

Amy shook his legs to get his attention. "We're playing spring."

"With dandelions?" He couldn't help but smile at the amusement in Darcy's face.

She turned her expression suitably sober, but her eyes continued to remind him of all life offered to the brave and free. To someone who hadn't vowed to guard his heart against more loss and pain.

Darcy nodded seriously. "Dandelions are the official badge of spring. Proves it's finally here to stay."

"Funny," he murmured, still stuck in the spell of her gaze. "I always thought it was the meadowlark." As if on cue, a bird trilled from a nearby fence post, and they turned toward the sound.

"Can't be. Not everyone gets to enjoy a lark. But everyone gets dandelions."

He chuckled. "Glad you didn't say enjoy them or I'd have to argue."

She flashed him a quick smile. "I believe we've proven they can be enjoyed." She waved a bouquet of yellow blossoms. "If the world hands you dandelions, make crowns and celebrate."

Blake again fell into the promise of her gaze, the promise of enjoyment found in ordinary things, ordinary events turned into celebrations. Amy diverted his attention as she lifted a dandelion wreath from her head and offered it to him.

"Bend over and I'll give you a dandelion crown."

He hesitated.

"Aren't you glad for spring?" Amy said, disappointment thinning her voice.

He saw the challenge and curiosity in Darcy's look.

"New life, new hope, new beginnings." She spoke softly, her musical voice reminding him of the meadowlark's song. "The Lord's mercies are new every morning," she said. "I never feel it more true than on a fine spring day like this."

To disagree seemed heretical after that. He bent and let Amy place the yellow crown on his head, then sat on the corner of the blanket. Again he met Darcy's look. "I'm not doubting what you say about new life. . .or God's new mercies, but. . ." He struggled to find the words to explain a fragile thought just out of his reach. Slowly he formed it into words. "New doesn't mean you're free of the past."

She turned toward the bird, singing his heart out. "Look at him. He's sitting on an old, splintered post surrounded by a mud puddle. But his surroundings haven't quenched his spirit or muted his song."

"I guess not. Is that your philosophy? Ignore the past. Sing and dance and pretend it doesn't exist?"

She twirled a limp dandelion for a moment, then met his gaze.

He allowed himself a fleeting sense of disappointment that

the warmth and fun in her eyes had fled, replaced by cool detachment, cautious defense.

"Some things a person can change. Others you just have to accept and move on or"—she paused—"or let them destroy you. I don't believe in letting the past and things I can't change or control rob me of the joy of the present." Her gaze turned to Amy.

Blake did not like the possessive look in her eyes.

She jerked back to face him. "Are we so different, really? Don't you have to move on from your loss and, dare I say, disappointment? Don't you have to choose to trust God for both the past and the future?"

He hadn't known she was a Christian, and despite himself he again fell into her gaze, knowing a click of instant connection based on their shared faith. He nodded slowly, his tongue thick and uncooperative. "I daily choose to trust God."

"Me, too." Her voice was soft as the dandelion Amy brushed against his chin.

She smiled, and he smiled back. A sense of something sweet and wonderful passed between them.

Amy hugged him, practically throttled him. "This is the happiest day of my life." She spun around and gave Darcy an equally exuberant hug.

Blake wanted to grab Amy and hold her on his lap. He wanted to keep her from Darcy. Keep her from being hurt. Yet he also wanted to capture the joy of this moment and lock it inside Amy's heart where she could pull it out after Darcy left and find comfort in it.

He stared at the green blades of grass poking up through the straw carpet of winter. He couldn't trust moments like this. They were too soon replaced by sorrow, loss, and regret. He pushed to his feet. "Come on, Amy. It's time to go home."

"Aww," Amy protested.

"You can come back anytime," Darcy assured her, and

apparently cheered by that thought, Amy raced across the yard.

Blake felt Darcy's gaze on his back as he strode away. He felt as if he had been on a wild bull ride of emotions. For one exciting moment he'd let himself feel things he hadn't allowed in a long time—joy, connection, anticipation. But reality was the thump when the bull landed on all four feet, the thud jarring up his spine into the base of his head. Reality was the workload that threatened to become a living avalanche, the care of Amy, and protecting her from further hurt.

Amy waited for him at the house. He swiped at the yellow dandelion butter on her cheeks. "You'll have to scrub really good to get that off."

She nodded. "I don't mind."

"Amy—" How did he voice his fears without robbing her of the temporary joy? "Amy, remember. Two weeks and then she's gone."

Amy sighed dramatically. "She's the best sister in the whole world."

Blake's neck spasmed. Amy was going to be heartbroken. And he seemed powerless to prevent it.

❧

Darcy pulled on her running shorts and a wicking T-shirt. She laced up her running shoes and headed out. She pounded down the dirt trail. So far she'd run three directions from the ranch. To the north she'd discovered a field of pale purple crocuses. South, she passed three home sites. One with a beautiful cedar log house, one with a sprawling ranch-style house, and the third with a tiny two-story box of a house badly in need of painting with a rusting collection of machinery filling the yard.

Today she ran west and found a wide river. She dipped her fingers in the water and discovered it icy cold from the spring thaw.

She turned down the road toward the ranch and laughed again at the sign over the gate. BAR T RANCH. Did anyone stop to think *Bar T* sounded like "party"? And no one here seemed to know how to have fun. Work was the defining quality as far as she could tell. She ran early in the morning so she could spend the rest of the day with Amy. Despite being nineteen years older, Darcy couldn't remember ever knowing such joy in another person. Daily she thanked God for bringing Amy into her life.

But no matter how early she went for her run, she saw Blake either out in the fields or hurrying across the corrals in long strides as if he had no time to waste. Except for Sunday. She'd slipped into the service late, not wanting to encounter Blake's unfriendliness. She'd slipped out during the closing song.

She looked around now. Yup. There he was. Climbing onto a tractor. Already hard at work.

He saw her and waved her over.

She hesitated. She didn't have to be overly brilliant to realize he'd been avoiding her the past few days—since the day he'd found her and Amy making dandelion wreaths. And to think she'd felt there had been a little connection between them, had been certain they'd shared something warm and sweet. A touching of the spirit and soul. Acknowledgment of a similar faith.

But it just showed how wrong she could be. About all they shared were his dark looks. She'd had her fill of his scowling at her or watching her as if he expected her to steal the land out from under his feet. She could pretend she hadn't seen him, but he waved again and called something. No way she could escape. She changed direction and jogged across the field toward him.

"Can you drive a truck?" he asked as soon as she was close enough to hear him.

"Sure. Why?"

"With standard transmission?"

"I've done it a time or two. Not very often," she added hastily in case he thought she was an expert.

"Would you mind helping me?"

She blinked and suddenly grinned. "Me?" She pressed her palm to her chest. "You're asking me—the girl most likely to annoy you—to do you a favor?" She laughed at the expressions of frustration and resignation crossing his face and wondered at the incredible lightening of her heart that he should turn to her for help. "Clearly you wouldn't be asking if you weren't stuck, but still it feels good." She gave a wide look around. "You sure there isn't someone else you'd rather ask?" It was a lot of fun teasing him, especially when he rolled his eyes and looked pained. And incredibly handsome, framed against the sun-bright sky, his brown hair haloed with sunshine. He wore faded blue jeans and a white T-shirt.

"Rub it in. But I'm stuck."

She planted her fists on her hips and grinned widely. "I will be so pleased to help you." She knew her tone conveyed just how happy she was to have him at her mercy—if only briefly.

"Why do I get the feeling you're enjoying this way too much?" He stood on the tractor step, grinning down at her.

"It's just nice to be needed." She stared up at him, caught by the warmth in his dark eyes. He enjoyed the teasing as much as she! She realized how long they'd been grinning at each other and jerked her gaze away. "What do you want me to do?"

"Can you follow me in the truck? I have to bring home some bales."

"Done." She jogged over to the vehicle and started the motor. She managed to remember how to clutch. She found the gear and jackrabbited forward.

Blake sat behind the steering wheel of the tractor, shaking his head and grinning.

She flashed him an okay sign, then followed him across the field and along a muddy trail until they reached a field with big round bales on it. He stopped the tractor and held up his hands to signal her to stop, pretending to be afraid. At least she thought he pretended. Yup. He grinned as she jerked to a stop.

He jumped down and pulled her door open. "Been awhile, has it?" His voice rolled with mirth.

"You have no idea." She jumped out and hurried around to the passenger side while he slid behind the wheel.

Just then his cell phone rang. He pulled it from his breast pocket, flipped it open, and said, "Hello." Darcy could hear a shrill voice. "Hey, squirt. What's wrong?"

Amy. Even from across the cab of the truck she sounded upset. Darcy shamelessly listened to the conversation. As if she had a choice. She couldn't make out the words, but obviously Amy didn't like something.

"Amy, just do what she says."

More shrill sounds from the phone.

"You know you can't do that. Behave yourself." He listened, murmuring, "Uh-huh," several times.

The shrill sounds diminished, so Darcy heard only a drone.

"I can't come home right now. You be good, and I'll see you later." He broke the connection.

"Problems?" Darcy asked.

He kept his attention on the trail as they bounced back to the farm. At first she thought he wasn't going to answer; then he sighed deeply and rubbed his palm along the steering wheel. "Amy doesn't like obeying Aunt Betty. It's been hard on her having so many changes in her life."

"I—" She'd been about to suggest she could take over more of her care. But, as he said, Amy had dealt with enough changes. She could understand his concern about how her visit would impact Amy. How could she assure him it wouldn't when it was a fear she shared? How could she ever say good-bye to her little sister? Yet she didn't belong here. She wouldn't be able to stay once her vacation was over. "I've enjoyed getting to know her," she said instead. "She's a spunky little thing."

Blake laughed. "She's been like that from day one. Maybe even before. She came two weeks late. Mom said we should have known then that she would do things her own way in her own time."

Darcy leaned back, watching the pleasure on Blake's face and wishing she could have been part of this charming little girl's life from the beginning. She chomped down on the bitterness rising in her throat. It was pointless to blame people now dead. She knew the past could destroy her enjoyment of the present if she let it. And she wasn't going to.

Blake slanted her a look full of warmth and humor. She knew it was because his thoughts were on Amy, but she enjoyed the way it made her feel part of something special. "When she was too young to talk, she still made us all understand she had her likes and dislikes. The bottle had to be just the right temperature or she'd give us an annoyed look and refuse it." He shook his head and laughed. "She was never afraid to try things. She was so determined to walk she was fearless. No matter how hard she fell, up she got and right back at it. She had bruises from head to toe. We used to worry someone would report us to the authorities."

"You sound as if you were very involved with her from the beginning."

His smile fled. "Mom was sick. She didn't know until after she got pregnant that her heart wasn't up to it. I guess she'd had some sort of virus infection that damaged it."

Darcy saw him stiffen and knew he was dealing with his private pain.

"She never recovered from having Amy. Yeah, I was there a

lot, trying to make things easier for her."

Darcy stared out the window, trying not to imagine an attentive, supportive Blake. Trying not to think how her life had been the opposite. She'd learned early to stand on her own two feet and not expect anyone to be there to help her. Her mom was too busy working, too restless.

They moved so often she had no close friends.

Her father had conveniently forgotten her. She had no siblings. Except now she did. She had Amy.

Blake sighed deeply. "Rob once said Amy reminded him of you. He said you were ornery as a child, too."

As a child. He remembered her as a little girl, but he didn't know her as an adolescent, an adult. And now he never would.

They stopped beside the machinery shed. He leaned his left arm on the steering wheel and studied her, his expression faintly amused. "I guess I should have been prepared that you would resist everything I suggested."

She ducked her head, unable to face his look without feeling disoriented. She didn't know if it was regret, unfulfilled wishes, or something else, but a deep longing created a hole in her thoughts. "I hope I've learned to pick my battles," she murmured.

Blake laughed, and she looked up to see his face creased with amusement. "I think you mean that to sound mature and reassuring, but I get the feeling it could also be a warning. If you want something bad enough, you're prepared to fight for it. Right?"

Surprised by the approval in his eyes, she could only nod.

He squeezed her shoulder. "You and Amy are a lot alike."

Her lungs tightened at the warmth of his big, work-hardened hand on her. Blood pulsed in her cheeks. Just when she thought she'd pass out from lack of oxygen, he pulled his hand away.

"Thanks for your help." He jumped from the truck and headed around to her side.

She shoved the door open and slid out before he could help. With a muttered good-bye she headed for her safe little house.

six

Blake watched her jog across the yard. The first time he'd seen her running, he thought it was an animal. He'd stared at her loping across the landscape, as smooth and graceful as any deer he'd seen. Her long legs ate up the miles. He tried to calculate how far she went every morning, but it didn't seem possible she ran more than five miles before breakfast.

But right now he didn't have time to watch Darcy. He had a ton of work to do. Some of it should have been done last fall, but with Rob sick and. . . Well, it just hadn't been done, and now he was playing catch-up.

He hooked up the flat deck and drove back to the tractor. He spent the morning loading bales and hauling them home. Normally he lost himself in the rhythm of work, finding a soothing release from worries and concerns, but not today. Each time he drove into the yard, he glimpsed Darcy. First washing the windows of the old house, polishing the place like a diamond. Didn't she realize it would probably be left uninhabited when she left? Unless he rented it out. Might not be a bad idea.

Next trip she sprawled on a new chaise lounge, a small table at her elbow, a book propped in her hands. The life of luxury. A word he hardly recognized. She disappeared from his line of vision, and he pushed away the weary ache behind his eyes.

Next time he passed, Amy sat beside her. They seemed to be busy looking at Amy's feet. Had she hurt herself? He almost braked. But then the sisters looked at each other and laughed. What were they up to? He wanted to stop and see, but he'd never get these bales home if he didn't keep at it. He studied Darcy's face. She always looked so happy, so cheerful. Even when he came down hard on her, she maintained her sense of humor. Driving by, he suddenly felt old and sour. Where was the mindless calm he usually got from working?

His stomach rumbled as the noon hour approached. But he didn't have time to stop for a regular meal. He snorted. When was the last time he'd enjoyed such a thing? He grabbed his cell phone. "Aunt Betty. I'll just pick up a couple of sandwiches when I go through the yard."

She didn't offer any opinion about his decision. Probably busy taking care of that ragged old cat of hers. The poor thing should have been put out of its misery years ago, but Aunt Betty nursed Missy along, giving her regular shots for diabetes and fixing her a special diet. The cat was fed better than he and Amy. Small wonder Amy hated the animal.

He blew out his lips. Life used to be so easy. Do his work. Enjoy his little sister. Enjoy meals his mom cooked or the ones he cooked in the house Darcy now owned.

He stopped to pick up his lunch. Darcy and Amy sat under the sprawling elm tree where Amy liked to play. A circle of stuffed animals surrounded them, and they giggled as Darcy made a tiny bear dance and talk.

Amy saw him and raced to his side. "Blake, see how pretty my toes are." She rocked back on her heels and tipped her toes upward, every nail painted a different color.

Blake laughed. "Rainbow feet."

"Yup. And now we're having a tea party with my animals."

"So I see. Have you eaten?"

She nodded solemnly. "Every bite."

"What was it today—tomato or vegetable?"

"Tomato." She raced back to Darcy and plunked down cross-legged in front of her. "Make Tiny Tim again."

Hesitating, Darcy shot Blake a wary look.

"Go ahead." Blake grinned. "I'd like to see Tiny Tim."

She huffed. "You just want to mock me."

He pressed his hand to his chest. "Me? I promise I won't mock you. A Tiny Tim imitation is quite a challenge."

She raised her eyebrows, then turned and picked up a red, loose-limbed bear. Her voice high and quivering, she swayed the animal back and forth and sang "Tiptoe Through the Tulips." Amy giggled and held up a brown bear.

"What's wrong with your voice?" she said in her best gruff bear voice.

Tiny Tim stopped dancing and squeaked, "What's wrong with *your* voice? Can't you talk normal, like me?"

Amy struggled to control her giggles, then moved her bear face-to-face with Tiny Tim. "You're very sick. You should see a doctor."

Darcy laughed and ruffled Amy's hair. "You're way too smart for Tiny Tim. He doesn't know what to say about that." Her eyes glistening with amusement, she shot a look toward Blake.

Grinning back, he felt a jolt of shared enjoyment of Amy.

Amy scooted over and climbed into Darcy's lap. "Was Tiny Tim really real?"

"He sure was. My mom used to sing his song when she was happy."

Blake needed to get back to work, but he couldn't tear himself from this cozy scene. Much as he hated to admit it, Darcy was good with Amy. Perhaps even good *for* Amy. She'd stopped moping about the house, complaining she had nothing to do. Of course, Darcy kept her amused with painting toenails and playing make-believe. But even he, despite his reluctance, could see the two shared a special connection. He spun away.

"What made her happy?" Amy's question stopped him. He turned back to the homey scene, wanting to hear Darcy's answer. He wanted to know why her expression had suddenly grown sad.

"Moving. She loved to move."

Amy shifted, getting more comfortable. "I never want to move."

Darcy laughed. "I might get tired of sitting like this."

"No. You won't."

Darcy looked at Blake and shook her head. "If Amy doesn't want it, it just isn't going to happen." They shared a secret smile.

Amy jumped to her feet and waved her arms in a big circle. "This is where I live. I'll never leave." She raced up to Blake. "Right, Blake? We'll always live here."

"That's right." He watched the way Darcy's gaze turned toward the house she now owned, her expression surprised. "This ranch has belonged to the Thompsons for four generations," he added for good measure.

"Am I a Thompson?" Amy demanded.

"You're a Hagen," he said.

"I want to be a Thompson."

"I guess, seeing as you're my sister, you're almost a Thompson."

Darcy brought her dark blue gaze back to him. "I've never had a house of my own."

"Enjoy it while you can." His voice was brittle. No way could she even think of changing her mind about the way things were going to be settled. "Gotta go, squirt." He hurried inside, grabbed the now-cold grilled sandwiches wrapped in plastic and headed back to work, mentally listing the number of trips left to make in order to clear the field, then planning the spring work. Stuff that kept him from thinking about anything else, especially emotional stuff.

But that nasty little feeling of impending danger wouldn't leave him.

Amy was going to be hurt when Darcy left. They just didn't need any more pain around here. He meant Amy, of course. No one else would be hurt when Darcy disappeared again as he was sure she would. *Lord, keep Amy from being hurt. Help me know how to protect her.*

❧

"I like to do jigsaw puzzles," Amy said in response to Darcy's questions about the things she did. Darcy yearned to know everything about her little sister. Much would remain hidden in the years she'd missed, but she discovered that Amy, in first grade, could already read very well. She loved make-believe and had a whole bunch of cats, but she couldn't have one in the house because of "Aunt Betty's stupid old cat."

"You want to do a puzzle with me?" Amy asked.

"I'd love to."

Amy grabbed her hand. "Come on. I have to keep them in my bedroom 'cause Aunt Betty says they're too messy."

Darcy hesitated. She'd never been invited into the other house but was dying to see where Amy and Blake lived—no, she scolded herself, she only wanted to see where Amy lived. She had no interest in Blake. Never mind that she could inventory his entire outfit: a faded-blue plaid shirt with the sleeves torn off, giving her lots of opportunity to admire work-muscled, sun-bronzed arms. Equally faded blue jeans, worn almost white across the knees. A wide leather-banded watch drawing attention to his masculine wrists. Cowboy boots, originally tan in color, she guessed, now scuffed to the color of dirt. Maybe the boots gave him the rolling gait. To top off the picture, he wore a black cap, the bill curled into a trough. It sat back on his head at a jaunty angle. The girls in the office would drool so bad they'd need bibs. If someone chose him as the poster boy for a tourism ad, Montana would be overrun with women of every age.

"Come on, Darcy." Amy tugged at her hand.

"I'm coming." She let Amy lead her into the house. Darcy stared in disbelief as she stepped into an open area that appeared to serve as cloakroom, back entry, and general storage.

Aunt Betty considered jigsaw puzzles to be too messy? Darcy would have been more concerned Amy would lose pieces in the jumble. Of course, it was the back entrance on a busy ranch. Maybe the rest of the house was neater. Cleaner.

Amy tugged her into a big modern kitchen. Darcy had to strain to imagine the black granite counter beneath the clutter and struggled to picture the stainless steel appliances gleaming.

A woman stood next to the fridge—no doubt Aunt Betty in the flesh. Darcy had managed to glean a bit of information about the older woman. Blake's mother's aunt, she had apparently left her little house in town to help Blake with Amy when Darcy's father became ill—after what, Darcy guessed from Amy's comments, was a succession of unsatisfactory nannies.

⁂

Aunt Betty opened a can of something that smelled decidedly fishy. Without glancing in their direction, she scooped the contents into a thick china bowl and bent to offer it to an animal. Darcy shuddered as she saw Aunt Betty's cat. The animal had long, shaggy hair.

Amy tried to drag Darcy from the room, but Darcy cleared her throat, determined to greet the woman who had the responsibility of caring for Amy. "Hello. You must be Amy's aunt Betty. I'm Darcy."

Finally the woman turned and nodded. "I've heard about you." She studied Darcy frankly.

Didn't that sound friendly? Darcy returned the stare, seeing a woman far older than she'd imagined. Probably in her seventies. Steely gray hair cut in a short no-nonsense, no-fuss hairdo. No makeup. Did women that age even use the stuff? Eyes, dark like Blake's. Suddenly the woman smiled, and the sternness fled.

"About time we had someone younger and more energetic

around the place. I don't mind admitting I'm not up to running after a six-year-old. The way I look at it is I've done my share of child rearing. And now I have my own interests." She dropped her gaze to Amy. "Did you bring your laundry down?"

"Forgot," Amy mumbled.

"Well, remember." Aunt Betty nodded briskly and turned back to stroking the cat.

This time Darcy allowed Amy to drag her away. She managed a glimpse into the living room as they passed. Cluttered with books, papers, and pieces of mismatched furniture. Upstairs, Amy's bedroom was as messy as the rest of the house.

Amy rushed over to a table and spread out a half-dozen puzzles. "Which one you want to do?"

"Let's get your laundry before you forget again." There seemed to be plenty of it, lying limply on the floor and bed. Darcy began to gather up the soiled clothes, piling them at the doorway as Amy groaned her protest.

"Let's make your bed. Are there clean sheets somewhere?"

"In the closet."

"Can you show me?"

With Amy's help she found the linen closet in the hall, just beyond a room with an open door. She glanced in. Black jeans hung over the back of a brown wooden chair, and a pair of shiny black leather cowboy boots stood as if Blake had just stepped out of them. His room smelled like grass and lemons and leather. Darcy could picture him pulling on jeans, brushing his hair with the brown-handled brush on the long dresser. She jerked away and selected a set of clean sheets.

Another door, closed, stood at the end of the hall. "Who sleeps there?"

Amy went to the door and opened it, hovering at the threshold. "Mommy and Daddy did. But I don't remember Mommy."

Darcy, curious, joined her at the doorway. It was a simple room, the bed neatly made with a forest green duvet, an earthy-colored area rug in the middle of the hardwood floor. A large framed photo of the farm hung next to the closet. Over the bed was a picture of the four of them—her father, Amy's mother, Amy, and Blake—looking like the perfect family. Amy must have been about two. Darcy could see the older woman already showed evidence of her failing heart in the dark shadows under her eyes. And Blake's look of adoration and determination showed he'd already shouldered his protective stance. She tried not to see how her father leaned over them, obviously loving them so much he could forget he had another daughter somewhere. One who'd been forced to grow up without that sort of love and acceptance. She looked into his blue eyes so much like her own and Amy's. She didn't realize they shared that with their father. Or had she pushed away the knowledge? She crushed the pile of linen to her chest and pushed resolve deep into her being. She'd learned a long time ago how to survive without her father. The only thing he'd ever given her was Amy.

She smiled down at her sister rocking back and forth on her heels, studying her painted toenails. "Let's go make your bed."

Amy talked as Darcy stripped the soiled sheets from the bed and remade it. The laundry pile grew larger as she added the sheets and socks she'd found tangled in the bedclothes.

"My favorite is the kitty puzzle. Do you want to put it together with me?" Amy asked, impatient with the delay.

"I'll make you a deal."

Amy looked wary. Darcy laughed. The kid had already figured out Darcy wouldn't be happy until the room was clean. She decided to sweeten the offer. "I'll do two puzzles with you if you help me pick up all these toys."

Amy gave her an annoyed look that made Darcy laugh again; then she screwed her face into an equally annoyed look, silently challenging her little sister. Amy pulled her lips down even harder, and then she laughed. "Okay."

Soon the room was neat, the shelves filled with books and toys, and the stuffed animals piled in the hammock attached to the wall. Darcy would have liked to dust and vacuum, as well, but a deal was a deal. Amy had done as agreed. So would she.

Two hours later they had finished all six of Amy's puzzles. Amy yawned. "Want to see my cats? They're lots prettier than Aunt Betty's ugly old thing."

"Sure." She scooped up the heap of laundry as she followed Amy downstairs. "Show me where the laundry room is, and I'll dump this stuff."

Amy led her to a bright sunshine-yellow room off the kitchen, and Darcy dropped her armload on the floor next to another pile. Seemed Aunt Betty wasn't in a big hurry to tackle the job. "I'll put a load in before we go outside," she told Amy.

The washer was full, and so was the dryer. She pulled out four pairs of Blake's jeans. Her face felt hot and prickly as she folded them and stacked them on the dryer, then blindly emptied the washer. By the time she sorted out the whites and dropped them in the machine, she'd convinced herself just how foolish it was to think about doing this on a daily basis.

&

They stepped into the barn, and Amy turned left into a room. Darcy breathed the strange smells—a combination of mushroom, ammonia, and some kind of disinfectant.

Cats sprang from every corner and raced in from the rest of the barn, meowing and wrapping around Amy, who plunked to the floor so they could crawl over her. She made sure to pet each one.

Darcy stopped at the doorway, reluctant to enter what was obviously Blake's domain. The whole room bore signs of his labors, carried hints of his scent, and gave her a warm, cozy feeling. She pictured him coiling ropes with his strong hands, hanging the leather halters on hooks, and smiling the secret pleased smile she'd glimpsed a time or two.

"Fatty isn't here," Amy said. She pushed the cats away and hurried to a wooden box. "She's had her babies. Look!" Amy almost screamed in her excitement.

Avoiding the cats tangling around her feet, Darcy hurried to see. "Ohh. They're so little. I've never seen brand-new kittens. Can I hold one?"

Amy looked deadly serious. "You better let me get one. Fatty knows me and won't mind if I touch her babies."

The mother cat meowed a warning as Amy lifted out a tiny black kitten and carefully transferred it to Darcy's cupped hands. The kitten nuzzled about, helpless and blind. Such tenderness engulfed Darcy so much that tears stung her eyes. "It's so tiny. I never imagined." She'd never seen a kitten that wasn't bouncing around playfully.

A cow in the barn lowed. A deep voice spoke soothingly.

"It's Blake." Amy raced to the door and yelled, "Blake! Blake! Fatty had her kittens! Come and see!"

Darcy didn't want Blake to witness how a tiny kitten made her feel mushy and protective. And helplessly vulnerable. Her reaction to the kitten was mixed up with regret at so many things—an odd emptiness she couldn't explain but which had been growing steadily the last few days. It sucked at her insides like a hungry yawn. She couldn't let herself be swallowed into that chasm. It frightened her. It mocked her. It made her want to run back to her own house, curl up under a fuzzy blanket, and pull it over her head until she felt warm and secure. *Lord, please give me Your peace.*

"Let's have a look." Blake saw Darcy and smiled. She pulled in a gulp of musty air and found calmness. The world righted itself.

He crowded close to her and bent over the box, murmuring

soft words to the mother cat, telling her what a fine job she'd done. "Five of them. Amy, if this keeps up, you'll have to get a job to pay for their feed."

Darcy recognized his teasing, but Amy took him seriously. "I can help you, and you could pay me just like you do Cory when he comes over."

Blake chuckled and ruffled her hair. "I was kidding. I think we can afford a bag or two of cat food." He picked up a mottled kitten, cupped it in his palm, and held it at eye level, chuckling when the tiny thing snuffled at his thumb.

Darcy thought she would choke at the sight of his large hands holding the kitten so gently. She turned away, pretending to study the kitten she still held. How silly to let five animals, each no bigger than a mouse, trigger so many emotions.

Blake returned the kitten to the box, murmuring reassurances to the mother cat, and then he stroked the one Darcy held, his fingers brushing hers. Her heart danced with a hundred different reactions. A longing for the tenderness he revealed. An ache to be protected the way he protected his loved ones. The need to belong to her father's heart as Blake had. She tightened her muscles to keep from jerking away, offering a silent prayer that she'd keep things straight in her head.

"All healthy and strong," he said. "Guess we'll have to keep them all, won't we, squirt?"

Amy nodded. "I'll take good care of them. I promise."

Brother and sister studied each other intently. A silent understanding flashed between them. Blake grinned. "I know you will." He glanced at his watch. "You'd better go get washed up for supper. I'll be there as soon as I look after a cow." He flashed Darcy a grin as he headed out of the room.

It wasn't until he disappeared from sight that Darcy could get enough air into her lungs to stop the dizzy feeling that descended at the way the casual brush of his fingers on hers had started a storm of emotions.

A few minutes later she and Amy parted ways, and Darcy headed for her house. She dropped to the old sofa and pulled around her a beige afghan she'd found in the narrow linen closet.

Her insides felt jumbled. She didn't like it. She had long ago learned some emotions were best ignored. Maybe she'd become too efficient at turning them off because it scared her to see the tip of so many unexplained feelings poking through the edges of her carefully constructed life. Part of her demanded she pack her bag and continue with her vacation right now before something erupted she didn't want to deal with. Another part, one she hardly recognized, demanded she stay and find out what lay beneath the surface. Truthfully, giving up her vacation didn't seem like a hardship. Not in the least. The ranch was a nice place to spend her time. The scenery superb. She pretended she meant the rolling hills and the distant mountains and the glorious sunsets, but all she pictured was Blake striding across the yard, adjusting his cap against the sun, hunkering down to touch the kittens, or ruffling Amy's hair.

Her chest felt as if something hot and heavy descended on it, making it almost impossible to breathe.

Okay, sure, she'd admit Blake was good-looking. In fact, she ought to buy one of those disposable cameras and take some pictures for the girls back at the office. But she wasn't interested in him that way. She couldn't be because of the wall of resentment that he'd been the one her father chose. She'd seen the look on her father's face in the picture hanging over his bed.

She'd also seen the look of tenderness in Blake's expression as he held the tiny kitten and ruffled Amy's hair.

She threw aside the afghan and jumped to her feet. This

was ridiculous. There was no room for her here.

𝕚𝕒

The next morning, as Darcy tied her running shoes, she watched Blake drive away. She spent the day with Amy, admiring the new kittens and playing pretend under the trees. After Amy reluctantly returned to her house for supper, Darcy headed for town.

She got enough supplies for the next few days and bought herself a large pot of flowers to put in the sunroom. If she were staying longer, she'd be tempted to redecorate it like an Italian villa with lots of wrought-iron furniture, some big pots of plants, and a few statues. She poked through the display in the hardware section. But she wasn't staying, so what was the point?

She would hate to sell her house. Perhaps she'd change her mind and keep it. She could use it for a vacation home. The girls at the office would be thrilled to share it with her. They could admire Blake firsthand.

Her insides knotted at the idea. She didn't want any of them drooling over him. She blinked. Was that jealousy? How absurd. How primitive. How infantile. She didn't even know how she felt about him. She'd enjoyed some fun moments with him. She'd been touched by the evidence of his soft side, but it was all mixed up with the thought he was the one her father chose while she was the one left out.

As she drove back toward her house, she saw a boxy gray car parked in front. She grabbed the wheel with both hands. She didn't know anyone who'd be visiting. Had she locked the door when she left? She'd been getting careless about it. Had Blake seen the car drive up?

A quick glance toward the barn and she knew Blake hadn't returned. Her shoulders sagged when she saw Aunt Betty drumming her fingers on the wheel, Amy bouncing up and down on the seat beside her. What was going on? She barely turned off the motor of her vehicle before Amy burst from the gray car and headed toward her. Darcy opened the door so she could hear her.

"Aunt Betty wants to know if I can stay with you."

"Of course." She grabbed her bags and headed toward the older woman, who rolled down her window.

"Blake was supposed to be back ages ago. He knows I have my sewing circle tonight. I told him from the beginning I wasn't going to give up my own interests, and he assured me I wouldn't have to. Now look what's happened. I'm going to be late, and he's nowhere to be seen." Aunt Betty frowned so deeply her face turned into a topographical map. "Seems like all he can think about is his work. Men can be so blind sometimes." She gave a mirthless smile. "If you don't mind watching Amy until he gets home. . . "

"Not at all." But she doubted Aunt Betty heard her as she shoved the car into gear and drove away.

Darcy laughed. "Can't imagine getting that excited about sewing."

Amy crowded to her side. "She made me go with her once. It's a bunch of old ladies sitting around talking. B–o–r–i–n–g. Then she got mad when I found some old books. I didn't mean to upset them on the floor."

"Of course you didn't." But Darcy could guess Aunt Betty wouldn't be anxious to take a restless child with her again. "Come on. You can help me put away groceries, and then I have to make my dinner. You can help if you want."

Amy ran ahead and threw open the door. Darcy promised herself she'd be more careful to lock it in the future. She set the groceries on the counter. Amy peered into the bags.

"Vegetables. Didn't you get any good stuff?"

"You'd be surprised how good vegetables taste when I'm finished with them."

Amy turned big eyes toward Darcy. "Whatcha gonna have?"

"Stir-fry steak. Have you eaten?"

Amy made a gagging sound.

Darcy leaned down to eye level. "Why do you do that?"

" 'Cause I hate macaroni."

Darcy hated to pump Amy for information about what went on in the other house, but she wondered about this unusual reaction every time Amy was asked about dinner. "Why do you hate macaroni?"

Again that gagging sound and Amy covered her mouth. Darcy got the distinct impression Amy's reaction wasn't fake. "It's all sticky. It tastes like—" She pressed her fingers to her mouth again.

"But surely there's something else to eat? What about potatoes or rice, vegetables or meat?"

"Aunt Betty says she doesn't like cooking."

The picture Darcy got was distressing. "How often do you get macaroni?"

"All the time."

Darcy made up her mind. "Why don't you help me cook my dinner, and then you can share it with me."

Amy looked doubtful. "Is it only vegetables?"

"And steak and rice. Has Blake eaten?"

"He didn't come home yet."

Darcy decided then and there to save some of the meal for Blake, ignoring the tremor of excitement the thought gave her.

But hours later Amy slept on Darcy's bed, and Blake still hadn't shown up. Darcy worked up a good head of steam as she waited. Finally the truck drove up to the other house. Blake went inside, emerged a few minutes later, and headed toward her place. Before he reached the steps, she had the steak strips frying. She could at least feed him before she tore a chunk out of his flesh.

&

At Darcy's invitation Blake stepped into the kitchen, his taste buds shifting into overdrive at the aroma of frying steak. Seeing her tight smile, he paused. Why did he get the feeling she was displeased? She couldn't possibly have a reason. He hadn't even seen her since yesterday in the supply room. He'd been far too busy.

First a cow had needed to be moved home so he could doctor her. He didn't like how thin she'd grown. Then he'd spent the better part of the day fixing fences. Some idiot cut the wires in several places—probably for the pleasure of snowmobiling last winter. Little did they care about the work and the dangers they caused. If he missed a spot, his cows could wander away. Even onto a road.

He and Rob had built that fence together, and as he repaired it memories assaulted him. Good memories, but still hard to deal with. It was one of those days when he missed the man so much it felt like a giant toothache.

And then Matt, the neighbor to the south, called to say someone left a gate down and their herds were mixed up. They'd worked until dark to part the cows into the right pastures.

On his drive home he'd been aching for a soft place to stretch out. He'd decided he was too tired to eat. Leftover macaroni had all the appeal of. . .

But as Darcy stirred the meat, his stomach gnawed at his backbone. He was hungry enough to eat anything. He quickly amended that. Anything but macaroni.

"You have Amy here?"

"She's sleeping on my bed. I've saved you some supper."

He swallowed hard. He couldn't tear his gaze away from the pan on the burner. "Sounds good, but I have to warn you I'm starving."

"There's lots." She scooped out the meat and dropped in a colorful array of vegetables. "Have a chair." She tilted her head toward the table.

He sat where he could watch Darcy. She moved with a smoothness reminding him of her grace when she ran. She was a woman easy on the eyes. He leaned forward, his forearms on the table. When had his feelings toward her shifted from antagonism to admiration? Perhaps when she'd been such a good sport about helping him? Or when she made him laugh as she played with Amy? Or seeing the gentle way she held the newborn kitten? When she'd shared bits about her faith? The jolt when his fingers had brushed hers as he stroked the kitten in her hand, the awareness of something far more than physical? To be honest, all of them made him open his eyes a little wider.

She pulled a bowl of fluffy rice from the microwave and put it in front of him, handed him a plate, waited until he'd scooped out a generous portion of the rice, and then slid the stir-fry mixture on top. He could barely swallow the saliva back fast enough.

"Go ahead. I hope you enjoy it."

His mouth was already too full to answer.

"Can I make you coffee or tea?"

"I'll take a glass of water if you don't mind."

She filled a tall glass with ice water and set it before him.

"Sit with me and talk."

"Okay." She sounded wary.

He gave her a good hard look. Did his presence remind her of all that wrong stuff she believed about Rob? He longed to clear up her misunderstanding. "I couldn't stop thinking of Rob today."

"Strange. I never thought of him once."

She obviously hadn't thought of him in years, but he didn't voice his thoughts. They'd been over that territory already. He needed to come at it from a different angle. "How come your mother and Rob got divorced?"

She blinked with surprise. "Because he left us."

"But why? There must have been some reason."

"Yeah. He didn't care about us."

Blake shook his head. "I don't buy that. That wasn't Rob. He was a devoted father."

"Huh. Try being a little kid wanting to understand." She leaned back into her chair and looked disinterested.

Blake couldn't tell if she pretended the look or if it was real, honed from years of believing what she said. "You need to get over your prejudice. It keeps you from seeing the truth."

Her eyes narrowed. "The truth about what?"

"About Rob."

"Blake, the truth is it appears he was a good father to you and Amy. But you have to accept he walked out when I was five and never once came to see me."

"It's a long ways from here to Seattle, and he was busy getting the ranch back on solid ground."

"A convenient excuse."

He hated to admit the reality of her words. Why hadn't Rob visited his elder daughter? He couldn't imagine treating Amy that way. "Why didn't you visit him?"

"Because I couldn't face any more rejection."

Did he detect her lips trembling? She clasped her hands together on the table, squeezing them hard enough to turn her fingertips red. He ached for the pain she constantly denied. He wrapped his hand around her cold fists.

"I'm sorry," he said.

She gaped at their hands, then slowly lifted her gaze to his face, her expression guarded, questioning.

"Sorry you've been hurt."

Her eyes turned cloudy. She looked so vulnerable he wanted to kiss her. Drive away all that uncertainty about being loved. This woman was made for loving. He'd seen it in the way she touched Amy, making her laugh, cuddling her at every opportunity. She was a woman full of grace and beauty. He saw it every time he watched her run. He saw it now in her trembling lips and the catch in her breath. He swallowed hard. "I'm sorry you missed having Rob as a father." His voice turned husky. "Sorry it's now too late to change things." He leaned forward, intent on capturing her mouth and kissing away all her hurt.

She jerked her hands away and sat up straight. Her eyes went from wide and warm to narrow and hard in a blink. "You're right. I can't undo the past. But I can speak to the present. You can't keep running from reality, burying yourself in your work."

Feeling as if he'd been thrown into an icy stream, Blake jerked back. "What are you talking about?"

"You're always working. Like a man possessed." She paused. "Or trying to outrun something."

"What? We were talking about you," he said. "Besides, I'm not running from anything. The pure and simple fact, for your enlightenment, is the ranch has been neglected for the better part of a year. I don't know what it's like in the city. Out here, if someone doesn't do the work—meaning me—it doesn't go away." He was on a roll. She'd hear all the hard realities of his life before he stopped. "It sits there waiting until I do it. So with a little imagination you can see I have twice as much work to do as normal." He glowered at her in angry defiance. "You make it sound as if I'm making excuses to be away from the house." Not for the world would he admit, even to himself, that he did prefer to be out working to being around the house, dealing with the constant reminder of the death and dying of the past several months. "The work has to be done. I have no choice." He told himself those words daily.

"I have no idea how much work you have to do or how long it takes." She shrugged as if it didn't matter. "But I do know a couple of things. First, you can't bury your emotions forever."

"You didn't hear a word I said. Listen to me: I am not

burying myself in work. In fact, if anything, the work is about to bury me."

She barely flicked an eyelid as she waited for him to finish, then went on as if he hadn't spoken. "Second, you have busied yourself almost out of Amy's life."

"You don't know—"

She held her palm toward him, ignoring his interruption. "Who would be spending time with her if I weren't here? You say she's well provided for, but"—Darcy leaned close, her eyes bright and challenging—"she needs more from you than a roof over her head. She needs your time and attention."

"You met Amy only a few days ago. What do you know about her needs?"

She returned him stare for stare. "I know what it feels like not to matter enough for someone important in my life to give me a few hours of his time."

They glared into each other's eyes, both breathing hard.

He shook his head. How had this deteriorated from wanting to kiss her to feeling an urge to strangle her?

He pushed to his feet. "Where's Amy? I'm taking her home."

She led him into the bedroom. He scooped his little sister into his arms. She smacked her lips twice, then burrowed her face against his chest. Fierce protectiveness burned through his veins. Darcy didn't know zip about his baby sister. Where was she when Amy was born? Where was she when Amy ran a high fever and had them all worried to death? Where was she when he and Rob explained over and over to Amy why her mommy was never coming home again? Where was Darcy when Rob died? She should have been at his side.

He strode out the door. "Thanks for supper and baby-sitting." Just before the screen slapped shut, he heard Darcy's soft words.

"You can't run forever, Blake."

Long after he'd tucked Amy into her bed and turned out all the lights and gone to his own bed, Blake lay staring into the darkness, mulling over the events of the evening. How had his attempt to help Darcy understand Rob gone wrong so fast? He dug his toes into the covers and jerked them down so they weren't bundled under his chin.

Sure, he was busy. Everyone understood that. Except, it seemed, Darcy. He had cows to move. Calves to process. Bales to haul. Fields to work. On top of that he had to go to a couple of auction sales, trying to find a good used rake. That didn't even take into account the paperwork waiting in the office, which he'd been putting off because it involved sorting Rob's personal stuff and clearing it from the office. Ahh. The paperwork. He could take care of two things at the same time. He flipped to his side and fell asleep.

seven

Darcy ran toward home. She'd added a couple of miles to her daily workout, building her endurance without undue effort. It surprised her how much she enjoyed running in the country. Today the fields were velvet carpets of brown and gold and silver. The sun shone in a satiny blue sky, unseasonably warm for April. She'd heard Blake muttering about a spring storm.

Blake. Last night ended in an argument. Not that she expected he'd be happy about her interference.

A swirl of dust down the road signaled a vehicle. It looked like Blake's. The truck pulled to the edge of the road and stopped. Blake swung out of the door. He leaned against the fender, his fingers tucked into the front pocket of his jeans, his cap shoved back as he watched her approach. At the warmth in his brown eyes her heart rate zoomed into the red zone.

She slowed her pace. What did he want? She'd seen the way he'd looked at her lips last night, knew he'd meant to kiss her. She'd stopped him by talking about Amy. Did he still want to kiss her? She faltered. Or argue some more?

He didn't speak until she drew abreast. "You're going farther every day."

She nodded, surprised he'd noticed. "I'm training for a race when I get back."

"I've been thinking about what you said. You know, about me being too busy. As I tried to tell you, I can't help it. There's just too much to do."

"Maybe you should think about getting help."

He nodded. "I've thought of it. Unfortunately, some of the

stuff can't be handled by strangers. You're family. Maybe you could help."

"Me?" she squeaked. When had he ever considered her family?

"Sure. You could sort the stuff in the office. Would you consider doing that?"

He'd invited her into his family? His house? What next? His heart? She pushed back the lurch of emotions at the idea. She allowed no dreams leading to futile hopes. Wasn't that the lesson she'd learned from her father? But there was no harm, no risk in helping Blake, giving him more time to spend with Amy. She wouldn't allow herself to think *she* might like to spend more time with him. *Lord, I trust You to help me protect my heart.* "Sure. I'll help if I can." She wiped her hand across her forehead.

He grinned, reaching out and brushing his fingers along her jaw. His gaze followed the path of his fingers. His hands had a roughness that caused her skin to tingle.

She couldn't breathe. Without conscious thought she leaned forward.

She let him tip her chin toward him, held her breath as he lowered his head. She allowed one flicker of hesitation, knowing this might change things between them in a way she couldn't control, and then she welcomed his kiss. She brought her hands up to his arms, reveling in the strength of his biceps. She admired a man with well-defined muscles.

He pulled back.

She swayed toward him. The touch of his mouth had warmed her lips, started a wash of emotions surging through her. She felt keenly the loneliness and longing she'd lived with all her life, wanting what she couldn't have, followed by a tidal wave of something warm and sheltering like finding a safe harbor. Blake. Her safe harbor? He was all she could hope for, a good man who loved his family. Uncertainty edged in.

What did Blake mean by this kiss? Was she a safe harbor for him? Or was it gratitude for her offer to help? Appreciation for the way she kept Amy amused?

She settled back on her heels. Forced her emotions back into a calm sea. She wasn't ready to ride the crest of that wave. She wasn't ready to open herself to the possibility of rejection.

He looked as surprised by the kiss as she was by her reaction.

They stood inches apart, gazing deeply into each other's eyes, searching, exploring, wondering. He smiled. "I'm off to town, but when I get back meet me at the house, and I'll show you what you can do."

"Okay." She watched his mouth as he talked, liking the way his lips flashed a smile.

He hesitated then climbed into the truck.

She waved at him in his rearview mirror. Without turning, he lifted his hand. She jogged slowly back to the ranch, grinning at a crow flapping by. Blake had kissed her. She liked it. Liked the feeling of being wanted. Her steps slowed. Was she playing house? Looking for something her father had denied her? Belonging. Home. Family. *Lord, Blake seems like such a good man, but I don't want to be substituting one ache for another. Give me wisdom to see clearly what I should do.*

She lengthened her stride, promising herself to be cautious.

By the time she showered and dressed in a pair of cool cotton shorts, a T-shirt, and a pair of matching flip-flops, all in teal blue, Amy was at her door.

She spent time with Amy, braiding her hair and reading her a book. At Amy's interest in Darcy's flip-flops, Darcy promised herself to buy her sister a pair next time she went to town. And maybe some new bright short sets.

Usually when she played with Amy, the little girl had her undivided attention, but this morning Darcy strained to hear

Blake's return. It was almost noon before he drove into the yard and parked by the big house.

"Let's go see what Blake's doing," she suggested to Amy.

Amy bounced out of the door and raced toward her brother. Blake braced himself and caught the little girl as she launched into his arms.

Darcy squeezed the bridge of her nose. The affection between the two was touching. She envied Amy her assurance of Blake's love. She slowed her steps. It was only because Blake was Amy's father figure. She was wondering what it would be like to feel such assurance of love from Blake as a man. *Be careful,* she reminded herself.

Blake smiled over Amy's shoulder as the little girl clung to him. "It took me longer than I planned. Seemed everyone picked today to go to town."

She nodded, her eyes feeling too bright. "I wasn't waiting." She was only curious about what he wanted her to do.

He unpeeled Amy and set her on the ground. "You can take these into the kitchen." He gave the girl two grocery bags. "You want to help?" he asked Darcy, holding out two more bags, one in each hand.

"Sure." She slipped her fingers into the handles, brushing her knuckles on his. The bags hung suspended between them. The moment froze as she looked into his eyes, a tiny pulse making itself felt high in her chest. She wondered if he felt the same disorientation she did.

"Got ice cream," he murmured. "It needs to go in the freezer."

So much for him being as bewildered as she. Obviously, he was not. It was only her unrelenting need to belong that made her think he might be. She took the bags and headed for the house, dropping them on the counter. Blake came in behind her, opened the side-by-side freezer, and stashed the ice cream.

"Where's Aunt Betty?" he asked Amy, who shrugged. "Aunt Betty!" he called, striding into the living room.

Darcy heard a sharp response, and then Blake returned. "She's on the phone with one of her cronies. Said she doesn't have time to make lunch today. She has to go into town and have lunch with a friend who's only here for a few hours. So. . ." He rubbed his hands together and looked gleeful. "We're on our own."

Darcy backed away. "I'll be back later then." She didn't wish to intrude.

Blake grabbed her wrist. "I'm hoping you'll have mercy on us and cook up a meal like last night."

Amy bounced up and down. "Please, Darcy. Cook us something."

"Anything but. . ." Blake grinned at Amy, and together they whispered, "Macaroni."

Darcy snapped her fingers. "That's exactly what I had in mind. Thick, gluey, yummy macaroni."

Amy gagged, Blake frowned, and Darcy laughed. "Just teasing. Seriously, what do you have in the house?"

"There's a whole freezer full of meat downstairs. Come on—I'll show you."

She followed him down to a large storeroom. Not only was the freezer full, but the shelves were well stocked, and a narrow door opened to a cold room with a solitary bag of potatoes.

"You have tons of food here."

Blake shrugged. "It's an old tradition on farms and ranches to keep in a good supply. I suppose it has its roots in pioneer days when you stocked up for the winter, but I know Mom always said we had to be prepared for a storm."

"I guess it's too late now to worry about that."

"We often get late snowstorms. We can be shut off from civilization for days at a time."

"You certainly wouldn't starve to death if you were. Why doesn't Aunt Betty use this?"

"She doesn't like cooking. She made that plain from the beginning."

Darcy poked through the contents of the freezer. "What do you want?"

"What can you do?"

From the supplies here she could cook up almost anything a person could dream of. But she knew he wouldn't want something four hours later. Something quick would have to do. "Hamburgers. Steak. Something with chicken breast?"

"Did I hear the word *steak*?"

"Steak it is. You want potatoes?"

"Yes."

A few minutes later they climbed the stairs again, carrying supplies. She had the impression the man was starving for a good old-fashioned meat-and-potatoes meal. So while Aunt Betty fussed about, gathering up her things and complaining she never had enough time in the day, Darcy peeled potatoes, thawed the steak, and prepared an apple crisp using a can of pie filling.

Both Amy and Blake hung about, drooling.

"Mom used to cook like that," Blake said.

Amy perked up. "She did?"

Blake nodded, his expression sad as he regarded his little sister. "You were too young to remember, but Mom loved to cook."

Amy tipped her head toward her brother. "Did I like what she made?"

Blake laughed. "You loved her mashed potatoes and gravy."

Darcy decided then and there she would make the creamiest mashed potatoes and richest gravy she could. With no fixings for a salad and no fresh vegetables, she chose three varieties of frozen vegetables and hoped they would pass the taste test.

Forty-five minutes later they sat down at the dining nook surrounded by a huge bay window providing them a panoramic view of the rolling fields and distant mountains. Blake uttered a hurried grace.

Amy tasted everything tentatively, her eyes growing wider with each mouthful. Blake, not nearly as cautious, filled his plate and dug in like a condemned man at his last meal.

Darcy accepted their words of praise. "I love cooking," she admitted.

"Like my mom," Amy said. She turned to Blake. "Did I like her potatoes and gravy better'n this?"

Blake chuckled. "I don't think so." He sent a warm glance to Darcy as if sharing secret enjoyment of this little girl. As far as Darcy was concerned, it wasn't a bit secret the way she felt about her sister. Amy meant more to her than she could have ever guessed. And Blake? Her gaze shot back to him. The jury was still out on that. Her feelings had certainly shifted toward him, but it was way too early to contemplate what that meant.

Everything was gone but little puddles of vegetables in the bottom of the bowls. Darcy took away the plates and serving bowls, and dished up generous portions of hot apple crisp with ice cream melting down the edges.

Blake sighed loud and appreciatively when she slid the bowl in front of him.

Amy glanced toward the adults. "Do I like this?"

Blake turned serious and shook his head. "I don't think so. You'll have to let me eat it for you."

Amy narrowed her eyes and studied him. "I'll try it first." She took a spoonful. Her eyes widened as she chewed. She smacked her lips and sighed, then leaned forward and wrapped her arms protectively around her dessert. "You can't have any of mine."

Darcy's gaze met Blake's as they laughed together. Enjoyment and peace slipped deep into her heart. She'd never been part of a warm family unit like this. Mom had always been busy and restless. Always heading for the next opportunity, the next great plan. Darcy knew this situation was temporary. She'd very soon—far too soon—have to go back to her real life. But just for a few minutes she let herself enjoy it, accepted it as one of God's generous gifts.

Blake finished his dessert first and poked Amy's elbow. "Looks like you need help." He winked at Darcy. Was he flirting with her? What was with that? It made her feel noticed. Special, even. After last night she'd expected disinterest, or anger. Did this mean her words made sense to him and he was grateful?

Amy tightened her grasp on her bowl and continued to eat.

Sending Blake a teasing grin, Darcy leaned forward and touched Amy's hand. "I gave you a large serving. You don't have to eat it all, you know."

Amy hunkered closer over her bowl. "I want to."

Blake leaned back, his arms crossed over his chest and watched. "You're going to explode."

Amy shrugged his comment away and plowed onward. Several minutes later, her bowl scraped clean and licked, she leaned back, patting her stomach. "I'm full."

Darcy looked at Blake, and they laughed.

He gathered up dirty dishes and carried them to the dishwasher. He stood close to Darcy as she washed the pots; then he took each item from her soapy hands and dried it. She finished and turned away, uncertain where to go, what to do next.

He dropped his hand to her shoulder, turning her toward the living room. "We have an appointment; did you forget?"

What appointment?

He led her down the hall and into a large room. A big oak desk sat in the center, a computer on one corner. Shelves lined two walls, filled with books and mementos. Large windows gave a view of the outbuildings and a glimpse of her house.

"The farm office," he said, dropping his hand to his side. "A lot of Rob's stuff is here. I haven't had time to sort it. That's where you come in. It would be a great help if you tackled the job." His voice sounded strained. "Maybe if his stuff was gone, I could face coming in here to do the farm books."

He wanted her to sort her father's stuff? No way. She didn't want anything to do with—

"It really makes more sense for you to do it than me. He was your father, so that gives you the right. And I'm sure you can do it with less emotional attachment than I could."

"Of course." Hadn't she told him often enough she had no feelings about the past? Why then did this suggestion bother her so much?

"Good." He jerked several boxes out of a closet and put them on the desk. "Most of his stuff is here."

"What am I supposed to do with it?"

He shrugged. "Whatever you think best. Anything to do with business, pile on the desk. Anything you think someone might want to keep, set aside for him or her. I guess you dump the rest."

She peeked in one box. It was filled with clippings and odds and ends. Nothing she couldn't handle. Yet her heart quivered, and she silently prayed for strength.

eight

For the first time since Rob died, the demands of work didn't keep Blake from returning to the house. He tried to tell himself he wasn't curious to see how Darcy was doing. As he stepped into the house, the aroma of freshly brewed coffee greeted him. Darcy stood at the pot, waiting for the amber liquid to drip through. Amy hovered beside her, chattering away about a card she held.

"Smells good in here."

The sisters spun around to face him. Amy rushed over, waving the card. "Look what Darcy found. A card I gave Daddy when he went to the hospital. I made it before I even started school." He bent to examine the homemade card she shoved at him. "Do you think Daddy liked this?" She twisted it around, appraising it. "It's not very good. Look how I spelled my name."

He took the card. "I remember when he got this. He was so proud of you. He thought you did a fine job for being only five."

Amy nodded. "I think I'll keep it."

"I suggested she frame it or put it in a scrapbook," Darcy said.

Amy looked serious. "We got any frames, Blake?"

"You can pick out one the next time we're in town."

She skipped away, her gaze on her treasure.

"I found the card in my father's things," Darcy said.

"I'm glad you thought to give it to her. It's made her happy." They regarded each other.

Blake sensed her wariness. Whenever the discussion turned

to Rob, she pulled back into herself, cautious, guarded. He'd hoped sorting Rob's things would help her see the good side of the man.

"How is it going?" he asked.

"It's slow. I feel like I have to check every item carefully to make sure I'm not throwing away something valuable."

He didn't ask if she meant valuable in a monetary sense or emotional. It encouraged him she'd seen the value of hanging on to Amy's card. She'd treasure it in the coming years.

"Coffee?" Darcy offered him a cup.

Normally he didn't bother with the stuff, but it smelled so good he couldn't bring himself to refuse. He took the cup from her, wiped a streak of dust from her cheek, felt her tense. Her gaze lifted to him, and he read the wonder. He edged forward until they almost touched.

"Blake! Blake!" Amy called. "Can we go to town now?"

He jerked back. "Sorry, squirt! Not today!" He gulped his coffee.

"Do you want to see what I've done?" Darcy asked.

He followed her to the office where neat piles covered the desk. A big green garbage bag squatted beside the desk.

"I threw out the old sale catalogues and flyers. This pile"—she pointed toward the desktop—"looks as if it might be farm stuff. I'll let you decide whether or not to keep it." She touched the box on the desk. "I think the first box was the easiest. There wasn't anything personal in it." She took a deep breath. "This box, however, seems to be mostly personal stuff." She lifted her gaze to him. "You sure you don't want to go through it?"

He shuddered. He couldn't face the painful reminders of the man he missed so much. "I'd sooner wrestle a bear."

She nodded, her expression troubled. "It's a lot harder than I thought it would be."

That's what he wanted. Wasn't it? For her to mourn the

man who'd been her father? Acknowledge he'd meant just a little to her?

She pulled out a picture and smiled widely, her eyes sparkling like sunshine on water.

He gave his cup of coffee a hard look. The caffeine had shot his heart into overdrive.

"I believe this must be you." She held the picture toward him.

He took it and groaned. "Naked as a baby."

She giggled. "You were a baby."

He read the inscription on the back. " 'Rob. This is Blake at six months. Cute or what? Love ya. Kathy.' " He flipped the picture to the desk. "Why would Mom give him this?"

She patted his shoulder. "Probably so they could have a good laugh. After all, what were you when she gave him this? Thirteen? Fourteen? And maybe a bit rebellious?"

"Not me. I didn't have time for that. My dad died when I was twelve. By the time I was fourteen I was doing a man's work."

"I guess you must have been glad when my father came along."

He heard the brittleness in her voice. "I was relieved to have someone else share the responsibility. I was happy he made Mom laugh again. But, Darcy, he didn't choose me over you. You have to believe that."

She stared hard at him. "Why?"

"Because—"

"It eases your conscience?"

"I don't need my conscience eased. I loved Rob and miss him like crazy."

"As I've said before, I'm sorry for your loss." She moved back to the desk and pulled out a handful of pictures.

"I'm no psychiatrist," he said, to which she arched her eyebrows. "But I think it's you who are running. Afraid to acknowledge the pain of losing him."

She smiled. "Nope. Because you see, I was forced to deal with losing him fifteen years ago."

"Surely you have some questions."

"Like what?"

How could she act as if nothing about Rob mattered to her? He wanted to force her to admit it did. "Like why he never came back?"

She nodded. "So now you're willing to acknowledge it wasn't my fault?"

He tossed his hands in the air. "You could have visited him anytime you wanted. No one would have chased you away."

"The same could be said for him."

"I give up. We just go round in circles."

"So why keep trying to convince me? Or yourself? The past is over and done with. I don't want to dwell on it. Or be stuck in it. I gave it to God a long time ago, and I don't intend to take it back."

&

The next day was Sunday, and she gladly turned her thoughts to church, thankful for a way to avoid thinking about the house across the yard, the office inside the house, the man who once occupied the office, and the younger man who now had all the responsibility of running the place. Her feelings toward her father and Blake had tangled inside her head. Going to church would help her get back on center.

The church building was as traditional as one could imagine, white siding with a tall spire. Darcy stood back to admire it, felt welcomed, her heart filled with peace. She'd declined an invitation to go with Blake, Aunt Betty, and Amy. She wanted to be alone and able to concentrate. She waited until just before the service to slip into a back pew. She saw Blake's back toward the front. Amy squirmed around and looked for her, lifted her hand in a quick wave when she spotted Darcy, and then, obeying Aunt Betty's warning look, faced forward and sat quietly.

Darcy had a quick look around. Easter Sunday and the front of the church overflowed with lilies. The worship leader greeted the congregation warmly, then announced the first song, one Darcy knew. She joined in the enthusiastic singing, her heart filling with praise and joy as she focused on God's love and provision. Bible verses Mrs. R had taught her came to mind as she sang. *"Never will I leave you; never will I forsake you. . . . The Lord is my helper; I will not be afraid. What can man do to me?"* Her confidence returned. Whatever she faced while on this visit, God stood at her side and would guide and direct her.

The pastor spoke further words of encouragement, reminding them of God's power in raising Jesus from the dead and what that power meant for each of them living a life of obedience to God.

She slipped out at the end, refreshed and renewed. She'd intended to leave without speaking to anyone, wanting nothing to shatter her newly regained sense of peace. Many stopped and welcomed her, however, and then Amy was at her side, Blake only a few steps away.

"How did you enjoy the service?" he asked as they left the building.

"Very much. Both the music and the sermon. And the people are so friendly."

"Will you be over later to tackle the office again?"

She quickly made up her mind. If he didn't work on Sunday, this would be a day for him to spend alone with Amy. "Not today." Due to Amy's teachers taking a couple of professional days following the vacation time, Darcy still had a few more days to spend with Amy before she had to return to school.

She spent the afternoon enjoying the sunshine, phoning Mrs. R and Irene, and missing Amy's enthusiasm and Blake's steadiness. How would she go back to the city and not see them every day? *Stop worrying about the future. Leave it in God's hands.*

🔊

On Monday she returned to the task of sorting her father's papers and facing the evidence that he'd had another life— one that hadn't included her. There was nothing new about that. She'd accepted the fact years ago. But pulling out picture after picture, letter after letter, memento after memento was like poking at a scabbed-over sore.

She hadn't seen Blake since yesterday at church. Somehow she'd let herself think he might hang around the house just to see her. As if. She pressed the heel of her hand to her forehead. Hiding out in this office, burrowing through papers, was getting to her. She'd again lost her mental equilibrium. *Lord, You are my strength and guide.*

Amy bounced into the room, upsetting a stack of calendars filled with notes. Darcy wanted Blake to decide whether or not to keep them. "Wanna play house?" Amy asked.

Darcy sighed. In her mind she'd been doing exactly that, imagining making meals for Amy and Blake, doing their laundry. She glanced out at the sunshine. She had to get out of here. "Why don't we go on a picnic?"

Amy danced up and down. "Goody, goody, goody."

Darcy guided her to the door. "Go tell Aunt Betty; then we'll go to my house and get ready." She'd make a simple lunch and take a blanket and some toys.

As they crossed the yard, Blake drove up.

"We're going on a picnic," Amy announced.

Blake smiled at his sister, then lifted his gaze to Darcy. "Where are you going?"

Darcy answered, "To the river west of here."

"Sounds like fun."

"Why don't you come with us?"

He shook his head. "Can't."

"Aww," Amy said. "You never play with me anymore."

"You have Darcy."

Amy nodded. "We'll have lots of fun, won't we, Darcy?"

"We sure will." She flashed Blake a tight smile. She hadn't honestly thought he'd tear himself from his work for an afternoon of fun and games, and she hid her disappointment. "Too bad you'll have to miss it." As she and Amy walked away, Darcy clamped her lips together to keep from pointing out that Blake was going to miss more than just a picnic if he kept it up. He was going to miss the most delightful years of Amy's life.

When their picnic was ready, Darcy drove down the road as far as she could; then they walked to the river.

Amy looked around. "Let's play pretend."

"Okay." Darcy realized she was getting pretty good at pretend. And not just with Amy. She'd allowed herself a few delicious moments of pretending she belonged here. Welcomed by Blake.

"Let's make a house." Amy directed her toward a shaded area surrounded by trees. Darcy draped the thick blanket she'd brought from home over a low branch, creating a tent, and they settled under it. Amy sat cross-legged, her hands resting on her thighs. "I think we're the first ladies to come here."

"Right. How did we get here?"

Amy spun a tale of a horseback ride away from home to a new area. Darcy smiled at her imagination.

The noise of a heavy animal sent a shiver across Darcy's shoulders. "Shh. Do you hear something?"

Amy's eyes grew round.

The sound came again. Closer. Heavy thuds on the gravelly ground. Darcy reached for Amy's hand, prepared to— She didn't know if they should remain motionless and silent or run for their lives.

The sound grew closer. Something brushed the blanket. Amy let out a squeak. A bulky shadow fell across the opening. Darcy screamed, then laughed in relief as Blake ducked down.

"Hi," he said.

Darcy giggled nervously. "You scared us half to death."

Amy, her eyes much too large, whispered, "I thought it was a bear."

"Sorry," Blake said, bending nearly in half to slip under the blanket and wedge himself between them.

He filled more than the space in the tent. He filled Darcy's thoughts, her emotions.

"So what are we doing in here?" he asked.

"We're pioneer women," Darcy explained, and Amy repeated her story. Darcy heard very little of the tale, thinking instead about how his arm behind her felt so warm and protective. He was a big man; yet he hunkered down around her like they belonged together. Which was too stupid for words. She scrambled out from under the blanket and sprang to her feet. "Let's go out in the sunshine."

Blake untangled himself until he stood. "It *was* a little too tight in there." He pulled the blanket off the tree, spread it close to the river, and stretched out, patting a spot beside him.

She eyed the narrow space and finally perched beside him, watching Amy spin around, chasing sunbeams.

"This reminds me of some books I read when I was a kid," Darcy said. "Something about a giggling brook and laughing trees. I liked pretending the things of nature were human."

Amy squatted in front of her, eyes sparkling with interest. "Tell me some more."

Darcy couldn't remember any more. "We can make up our own. See the sun flashing off the ripples like eyes winking? Winking river. Or"—she pointed to the leaves—"they're telling each other secrets. Whispering leaves."

Blake leaned on his elbow. "My dad used to bring me here. I'd forgotten all about it. We floated bark boats."

Amy bounced up. "How? Show me."

Blake pushed to his feet and strode toward the trees. He showed Amy how to select bits and pieces of wood; then they went to the river and had boat races, Amy squealing with excitement.

Darcy found a piece of bark and joined the race, yelling and screaming as her boat crossed their arbitrary finish line ahead of the other two. "I win! I win!" She grabbed Amy's hands and danced around with her. Blake's boat had been last. She danced Amy up to Blake and chanted, "You lose. You lose."

Blake jammed his fists on his hips and gave her a mock scowl. "Nobody likes a poor winner. Besides, what kind of example are you setting for little Amy?"

"A fun one?"

Amy dropped Darcy's hands, crossed her arms over her chest in a militant stance, and glowered at Blake. "I'm not little. When are you going to stop treating me like a kid?" She stomped away.

Blake stared after Amy as if she'd developed two heads. "Where did that come from?"

Darcy whooped with laughter. Her little sister certainly had a good dose of moxie.

Blake's deep chuckle joined hers.

After that, they couldn't seem to stop laughing. They played a game of tag with Amy. Then they walked, three abreast, along the river. Amy broke away to pick up shiny stones.

"This was a real good idea," Blake murmured as they watched Amy filling her pockets with rocks. "I can't believe I haven't been here since Dad died. We used to come often."

"Maybe it's time to let yourself have some fun once in a while." He didn't answer, and she continued softly. "I understand life hasn't been easy for you. You've had to shoulder far too much responsibility far too young. But you can't let it keep you from enjoying life at the same time."

"I thought I was until you came along."

"Oh, dear. That doesn't sound good."

"Believe me, it is." His stomach rumbled. "Did you bring enough food for me, or should I go home for lunch?"

"There's lots." She'd give up her own share if it meant he'd stay a bit longer.

They called to Amy and headed back to the blanket. Darcy divided the sandwiches and handed out boxes of juice. She was glad she'd baked cookies the night before and had generously filled a bag.

After they'd eaten, Amy sat at the edge of the river and tossed rocks into the water. Content with life, Darcy lay on her stomach next to Blake.

"A person could get used to living in the country," she said, then wondered where the thought had come from.

"I can't imagine living anywhere else," Blake murmured. "My great-great-grandfather, Cyril Thompson, came here before the government opened up the land for settlers. He had a thousand cows roaming freely. He built a log house for his wife and family."

"Sounds like Amy's story." She couldn't imagine roots going down four generations. The longest she'd ever lived in one place was the last three years in her own little apartment.

"My grandpa used to tell me all sorts of stories." Blake leaned on one elbow so he could look at Darcy. "I don't know how many of them were really true."

"Like what?"

"Well, he had this one wild story about a man who lived in the mountains. He used to point to a place where you could see a bit of valley and say, 'Right about there.' He said the man kidnapped a young woman right out of her own yard with the intention of forcing her to become his wife."

Darcy gasped. "Why would he do that? Did she get away?"

"Story goes he brought her back. I guess she wasn't too cooperative."

"Poor girl."

Blake chuckled. "Maybe poor man. But in the end they did marry. It seems the man had a scar on his face he thought made him ugly and figured the only way to get a wife was to force someone to marry him, but it seems the young lady saw past his scar to his heart."

"How romantic."

"Yes, indeed."

She narrowed her eyes and studied him. Was he mocking her? "Don't you believe in love?"

"Of course I do. I just don't think it has to be so dramatic. With my parents and with Rob and my mom, I saw it more as deep and steady. The kind of thing that's like a solid foundation."

Darcy studied the rippling water as unfamiliar longing washed through her. Blake knew where he belonged. And always had. He knew where he'd be at the end of his life. Right here with his children and grandchildren gathered around him. Darcy shook her head.

"What's the matter?" Blake asked.

"It's just so foreign to me. I can't imagine a place that's been in the family for generations. I can't even remember all the places I've lived." As to love that formed a foundation—well, she knew it existed. And she dreamed of the possibility in her own life, but she didn't have the calm assurance it was ordinary and expected. Not like Blake. For her it was a dream, and she'd learned long ago not to put too much hope in dreams. "Not everyone wants that sort of belonging. The very idea would give my mother hives. She liked moving on a regular basis. I think she found it exciting to look for a new place and welcomed the challenge of negotiating all the details."

"How about you?" His voice was low, serious, as if this were more than casual conversation.

She slid a quick glance at him, seeing the warmth in his chocolate-colored eyes. Then she forced her gaze back to the river.

"How do you feel about staying in one place?" His voice was soft.

She didn't answer right away. She was thinking of the house her father had left her. The idea still seemed impossible. She wanted to clutch at her ownership like a child refusing to let go of the penny needed to make a purchase. She didn't belong out here, even though she felt drawn to the place. And the people. Especially Amy. And, yes, Blake. But long ago she'd learned how disastrous it was to pin her hopes on one person, expecting him to provide her security. She'd learned to stand on her own feet and trust God for what she needed. She had a good, satisfying job back in Seattle where she knew what was expected of her. And she wasn't about to let any of her coworkers and friends down. She'd return. Run the half marathon and win it. And she'd resume her duties.

Blake got tired of waiting for her answer and dropped his chin to his hands. "I guess belonging doesn't appeal to everyone."

She didn't respond. How could she begin to explain the difference between them? The difference between knowing and dreaming.

nine

Darcy woke from a sound sleep and lay staring into the darkness. What wakened her? She strained into the silence. Usually she could hear the fridge or the clock on her bedside table. But the numbers on her clock had disappeared. She reached for the lamp and flicked it. Nothing. The power must be off. She shivered and snuggled deeper into her covers. And then she heard it. The roar and moan of the wind. A storm. Already the cold was enough to make her feet cramp. She supposed it would be a good idea to light a fire in the fireplace.

She gathered the bedclothes around her and padded into the living room, stumbling into the couch in the darkness. She'd seen a flashlight somewhere but didn't have a clue where and knew she'd never find it in the dark.

The fireplace was hard to miss, though. She stubbed her toe on the hearth and dropped her covers as she grabbed the offended member of her anatomy. The cold hit her like a blast, and she fumbled for the blankets.

She found the stack of wood to the right of the fireplace. A log rolled off and dropped on her foot. Darcy grunted, but this time she wasn't dropping her covers. She managed to open the fireplace screen and jab the log in.

Great. A fireplace and a log. But what she really needed was a fire. Which required matches. She patted her hips and chest as if she had pockets that might contain matches or lighter and giggled. Here she was doing the macarena alone and in the middle of a cold, dark night.

She edged her way to the couch and cuddled up under the

blankets. It surely wasn't cold enough to pose any real threat, but something shivered across her neck and raced down her spine. She recognized the feeling as intense loneliness. She laid her head against the back of the couch. Suddenly she sat up. No way was she going to let it get to her. She marched back to her bedroom, bumping her shins on the corner of the coffee table and then banging her head into the door, but she only muttered under her breath. She pawed through her drawers and found a heavy sweater, pulled it over her head, then found jeans and warm socks. Reaching out until she found the bed, she sat down to pull them on. She toed her way into her shoes, giggling as she tried to put one on backward.

She found her way to the back door and pulled down a heavy coat from the hooks. She caught a hint of Blake's scent as she burrowed into it. It took a few minutes for the icy lining to grow warm.

She'd survive. As soon as morning came, she'd find matches and start a fire. It would be an adventure.

How were they managing up at the other house? Was someone making sure Amy was warm enough? She could imagine Amy curled against Blake's chest, warm and cherished. A long, slow ache filled her. Try as she might, she couldn't dismiss it as cold. Truth was, she felt shut out. Unwanted.

She stamped her feet to warm them. She wouldn't allow self-pity. She recited verses Mrs. R encouraged her "girls" to memorize. " 'For all have sinned and fall short of the glory of God' " might not be the most comforting passage. She mentally shifted to the psalms. Chapter 23. The shepherd psalm. " 'The Lord is my shepherd. . . .' " By the time she'd recited the whole passage, her fear and loneliness subsided. She would never be alone. She had God's comfort.

She edged toward the window, hoping for a glimpse of the house. Did she see a faint flash of light? She strained into the darkness. It had to be her imagination. That was one thing she shared with Amy—an all-too-vivid imagination. And blue eyes, though she doubted hers were as lively as Amy's. Plus a stubbornness that could cause others to grind their teeth.

She smiled into the unrelenting darkness. It was tons of fun to share similarities with a little sister.

She heard feet stamping on the wooden deck, the sound muffled by snow. Her city instincts kicked in, and she shrank back, fearing an intruder.

But she wasn't in the city. She was on the Bar T Ranch. And who would wander around in a blackout and a raging storm?

The door rattled as someone tried to open it.

"Darcy, open up! It's cold as the North Pole out here!"

"Blake?" she whispered. "I'm coming!" she called, not caring a bit that she cracked her knee twice in her rush to unlock the door.

Cold, like a blast from the Arctic, hit her in the face, and snow stung her eyes. Blake shone a light in her face, then shoved her aside and pushed the door closed.

He stamped his feet and brushed snow off his coat. "Are you okay?"

Little tickles of warmth, like the first cup of morning coffee, filled her. "You came out in this storm to check on me?" It was the cold making her voice so husky. Yeah. Like she believed that. She wanted to hug him for his concern. Except for his snow-covered coat. She stepped back from the cold coming off him. "I'm okay."

He again shone the light in her face. She closed her eyes until he lowered the beam over her. "I see you found my old coat." He chuckled. "I haven't worn that in ages. I outgrew it. Looks good on you, though."

From the glow of his flashlight, she could see his face in

sharp planes, his wide smile, his hair hidden under a shaggy fur hat, and she giggled. "Has the wind blown us to Russia?"

He touched the hat. "You mean this? You like it?"

"Very aristocratic."

"Thank you." He bowed deeply. Then grew serious. "I wondered if you'd get a fire going."

"I'm not much of a Girl Scout. I wasn't prepared. And I couldn't find any matches." She patted her pockets again.

"The forecast is for the storm to last three days. No point in you trying to keep warm here. You might as well come up to the other house. We have a roaring fire in the fireplace. It's reasonably warm. Grab a few things, and I'll take you over. That way I can be sure you're okay." He pulled another flashlight out of his pocket. "While you do that, I'll crack open the taps so the water won't freeze."

She hurried to her room, humming as she threw some clothes and toiletries into a small bag. He cared enough to rescue her.

Blake was standing in the middle of the kitchen when she returned. She shone her light in his face. He turned aside to avoid the brightness.

"All ready?" he asked. At her nod he took her hand and pulled it through his arm. "Hang on, and whatever you do, don't let go. I wouldn't want to lose you out there."

She wouldn't want to get lost. And she certainly didn't mind keeping her arm tucked into his.

They stepped outside into a wall of snow and wind. She forgot everything but hanging on for dear life as they walked head-on into the storm. How did Blake know where to go? Fear made her stumble. What if they got lost? How long would they wander out in this wretched storm before they were buried in snow? Would they lie there until spring thawed out their lifeless bodies? *The Lord is my shepherd.*

Blake pulled her closer and forged ahead. She clung to him

and trusted he knew the way.

The pressure of the wind stopped so suddenly she almost fell.

"We're at the house!" Blake shouted in her ear. "We're out of the wind here." She stumbled inside. He closed the door firmly after them. A battery-powered lamp provided a golden glow.

She slipped out of her coat, shook it before draping it on a hook. She pulled off her boots and stuck her feet in her slippers as he shrugged out of his coat.

"Come on. Let's get in where it's warm." He took her hand and drew her past the dark kitchen into the living room where a fire roared and crackled in the big stone fireplace. Amy slept on the love seat. Aunt Betty lay on one couch, her eyes closed.

Blake didn't drop her hand until they stood facing the fire; then he stretched his hands to the warmth.

Darcy did the same. "Fire," she murmured. "Man's greatest invention."

Blake looked around the room. "Everyone is safe and sound."

Darcy stared into the flames. Was that all it was for him? Taking care of responsibilities?

Blake reached over to the end of Amy's couch and picked up a stack of blankets and a pillow. "You might as well get comfortable. We're here for the night."

She glanced around the room. One couch and a recliner left.

"You take the couch," he said.

"I couldn't do that. I'll take the recliner."

"No, I need to keep an eye on the fire." He made a bed for her. "There you go."

She felt uncomfortable. "I'm not really tired."

"Would you like something warm to drink?"

"How—"

He lifted an old kettle off the hearth. "Fire. Man's greatest invention."

She grinned.

"Hot chocolate?" he asked.

"Sounds good."

He brought two mugs and instant drink powder from the kitchen. He pulled the couch around so it faced the fire, and they sat with their feet propped on the hearth.

"Maybe the pioneers didn't have it so bad." She sipped the hot, sweet drink. "This is kind of nice."

"It's inconvenient if it lasts three days."

"Could it really?"

"Been known to happen."

"Amy's snoring. She sounds like a kitten purring." She met Blake's gaze, and they chuckled.

Aunt Betty shifted on the other couch and groaned.

Darcy settled back against the couch. She stared into the fire. "This is like camping, only cozier. You know, with the couch and everything."

"Have you done a lot of camping?"

"I once went to a summer camp in a wilderness area. But I never learned to be Ranger Sue. The only way I can start a fire by rubbing two sticks together is if one of them is a match."

He chuckled. "So you failed the survival skills test?"

"I never even qualified for the test. They begged me to pretend I hadn't taken the course. They offered me a lifetime membership to the shoppers' club if I kept it a secret. I suppose you have all your Boy Scout badges?"

"Nope. Didn't even go. But I can change the oil in a tractor in record time. And I can find my way from point A to point B without a map."

"From what I hear that isn't so much a skill as a denial mechanism for men."

"You think I'd sooner wander around lost than ask for directions?"

"Would you?"

He got up, put wood on the fire, and made them more hot chocolate, then faced her, leaning back on his heels, backlit by the glow of the fire.

"I might not bother if it was just me, but I would never drag around Amy or someone I care about. For their sake I would certainly ask directions."

She couldn't see his eyes, but she suspected they were hard and determined. He took this protective business seriously.

He'd included Amy in his cared-for category. She wondered who else he'd include. Aunt Betty, for sure. Maybe her? After all, he'd come to rescue her from freezing to death. Okay, maybe that was a little too dramatic. But he'd cared enough to bring her to a warm place. Was it just responsibility? Or was it more? Like caring?

He sat beside her again, and the conversation returned to camping. He told of trips with his father and then later with Rob.

Darcy tried not to think how Blake enjoyed the father things with Rob she'd been denied. She no longer blamed Blake. But she was grateful when he switched the topic to something else. She loved listening to him. The way his voice filled with pride as he talked about belonging to a beef club and showing his first steer. She laughed when he told how his dad saved the day when his steer got loose and headed for home.

Suddenly he turned so he could look into her face. The flame caught in his eyes and seemed to go deeper, as if burning into his soul. "I just realized something. I haven't talked this much about my parents and Rob since—" His mouth pulled down at the corners as he stared at her. He blinked. "Well, I suppose since my dad died. I didn't want to talk about it because—" Again he paused and searched her face.

Darcy held his gaze steadily, wondering what he sought and if he would find it in her or be disappointed.

ten

Blake's smile deepened, and pleasure spilled through Darcy. "I guess I was afraid of my feelings. Losing the three most important people in your life is overwhelming. I don't know when my good memories of them became more powerful than the pain." He touched her cheek, and the warmth inside her rushed to that spot like iron filings to a magnet. "Thank you for helping me see that." He settled back, sighing. "I know I won't ever stop missing them, but there are so many good things to remember."

"Tell me more about Amy as a baby."

He chuckled. "She never lacked for attention with three doting adults, but Mom insisted she had to accept certain boundaries. She was right. That early teaching has made Amy a good kid."

"How did she handle losing both her parents?" She wanted to know if Amy blamed herself. Did she feel abandoned?

"In both cases we knew ahead of time, so Mom and Rob took care to prepare her. I guess it helped. She didn't quite grasp Mom's death, but when Rob died—" He broke off and rubbed the bridge of his nose.

Darcy reached for his hand. He turned his palm up and held on.

"She took it a lot harder. She cried for about three days. After the funeral she retreated to her room and refused to talk to anyone, but I heard her talking to her stuffed animals. I let her be. Then she seemed to be okay, but she has nightmares."

"It's an awful thing for a child her age to face." Darcy was doing her best not to let her own feelings get mixed up with her sister's. Darcy's loss was in the past. Gone. Forgotten. Forgiven. Erased by God's love. Yet at times still very much alive and full of sharp edges.

Her daddy had left because—Darcy always feared it was because of her. She hadn't been good enough, smart enough, happy enough. Her rational self said it wasn't the case. But that other side, the one that insisted on dreaming impossible dreams, still wondered quietly and insistently. *Why wasn't I good enough?*

"Amy knew she was loved." Her voice felt impossibly tight, a sure giveaway she was letting her emotions get out of hand. She hoped Blake wouldn't be able to tell.

He jerked away. "Amy is still loved." He sounded fierce. "She will always be loved."

"I didn't mean—" She'd only been thinking of her father. No. Truth was, she was only thinking about herself, and she was deeply remorseful. "I'm sorry. Of course she is. It's obvious how much you care about her. I do, too."

He stiffened.

If she hoped to avoid a confrontation on the subject, she needed to find a new topic real quick. "Do you often get storms like this in April?" she asked.

"Once in ten years is too often in my opinion. But they aren't unexpected. This is Montana. And we're close to the mountains. Three years ago we had a major storm in May." He went on to describe it, and she settled back, enjoying his stories and grateful to have sidestepped an argument about her role in Amy's life.

As Blake told about a storm that brought a tree down, destroying the house his grandfather had been raised in, Amy started to cry.

They both jerked to their feet and rushed to her. Darcy held back as Blake shook the little girl gently. "Amy, honey, wake up." He glanced over his shoulder to Darcy. "One of her nightmares." He scooped Amy into his arms, talking to her softly.

Darcy knew the minute Amy woke up. Her cry ended in a gasp. She stared into Blake's face and then, sobbing, buried her head against his shoulder. He carried her to the couch and sat rocking her and murmuring softly.

Darcy sat beside them, aching to ease Amy's pain, but all she could think to do was rub her sister's back and add her voice to Blake's.

After a few minutes Amy's sobs stopped. She spoke around hiccups. "I dreamed I was stuck in a hole. I kept calling and calling Daddy. He just stood there and didn't help me. Why wouldn't he help me?"

Blake held her close. "It was just a dream."

Darcy's eyes stung. Try telling a child his or her dreams didn't mean anything. She couldn't forget a similar dream. Only she was trapped in a box. And no one answered her cries. Her mother assured her the dream meant nothing. But at six Darcy had known it did. It meant nobody cared. She pushed the memory away. "Amy, honey. It's okay. It's your mind telling you how much you miss your daddy. He can't be here to help you anymore, but Blake is. If you need something, you call Blake."

"I'll be here for you," Blake said.

Amy nodded. "I miss Daddy."

"Of course you do." Blake cupped her head in his big hand and pressed her cheek to his chest. "I do, too."

Amy grabbed Darcy's hand. "Do you, too, Darcy?"

There was no way to explain she'd stopped missing him years ago. "Of course I do, sweetheart." Her throat clogged with tears. She missed him in her own way. But she didn't dare dredge up those feelings of abandonment. They were too vicious. *Please, God. Help me remember that You care. You are a Father to the fatherless.*

Amy fell asleep again, and Blake put her down and covered her. Darcy returned to the couch while Blake tended the fire. She must have fallen asleep because she woke when Blake got up to put more wood on the fire. She lay stretched out on the couch, a blanket over her. She sat up and peered over the back. Amy slept in the love seat.

"Go back to sleep," Blake murmured. "Everything is okay."

And, believing him, she lay down and slept.

🙶

Blake struggled from his sleep and slipped from the recliner to put more wood on the fire. Amy hadn't wakened with another dream. Aunt Betty moved restlessly on the couch, coughing now and then. Darcy lay on her side, her dark hair loose around her face.

Everyone was safe from the storm.

Darcy sighed and shifted. For a moment he thought she looked at him; then the fire flared, and he could tell she slept. Even with her eyes closed, her resemblance to Amy was strong. But Darcy was even more like Rob than Amy. Why had there never been contact between them? There must be more than Darcy admitted or knew.

Aunt Betty coughed again and moaned. Darcy sat up and looked about her, confused. Then she yawned and stretched like a cat.

"Is it still storming?" she murmured, her voice thick with sleep.

"Yep."

Aunt Betty struggled to sit up. "My throat is very sore. Is there something hot to drink?" She swayed, moaned, and lay down again. "I'm sick."

Great, Blake thought. Do your best to take care of everyone, but there was so much you couldn't protect them from.

"I'll get you something," Darcy said, pushing to her feet. "What would you like?"

"Lemon tea," Aunt Betty croaked.

Gray light struggled through the windows as Darcy went to the kitchen to find the things she needed to meet Aunt Betty's request.

Blake headed after her but only made three steps before Amy woke, crying. "My throat hurts."

He turned back to comfort her. "You and Aunt Betty are sick."

Amy whimpered. "Where's Darcy?"

Darcy called from the other room. "I'm here! Would you like a nice hot drink?"

Amy tried to speak but grabbed her throat and nodded instead.

"That's affirmative!" Blake called. "There's lemonade mix on the lazy Susan! I'll fill the kettle!" He poured from the supply of bottled water and hung it over the fire to heat.

Together he and Darcy prepared hot drinks.

"What about food?" Darcy asked as they huddled side by side on the couch. "We'll need to eat."

"What can we do over the fireplace?" He promised himself he'd get a new generator the next time he went to town. He wouldn't leave himself or his family exposed to such hardship again. Family? Amy and Aunt Betty were his family now. And Darcy? He liked the idea of her being family, but she'd be gone once her days off were used up. What were the chances they'd see her again? Not very likely, if her past was any indication. He mentally pulled his family circle tight, leaving Darcy outside. He liked the woman, but he had no room in his life for a leaving kind of girl.

"If you have a big pot to hang where the kettle is, I could boil eggs for breakfast and make soup for later," Darcy said.

"Sounds like just what we need." He glanced at the two sick people behind him. When Darcy started to get up, he grabbed her hand and pulled her back down beside him. "Finish your tea first. There's nothing I can do for the cows until it's over. And I put out enough feed for the animals in the barn so that they're okay for now. We have all day."

He found a suitable pot. She boiled eggs while he toasted bread over the fire. They offered a nice breakfast to both Amy and Aunt Betty, who nibbled at their soft-boiled eggs, then pushed away the rest.

"I should feel guilty about being so hungry when they're sick," Blake murmured as he chowed down.

"But you don't." Darcy laughed. "And neither do I. I only hope I don't get what they have."

They finished and stacked the dirty dishes in the dishwasher. Darcy checked the two patients and passed out acetaminophen tablets. Both settled back and fell asleep.

Darcy filled the pot with a mixture of vegetables, tomato juice, and sausage, and left it to simmer over the fire. Delicious aromas made Blake's mouth water.

Darcy yawned and stretched. "Now what do we do?" She looked around the room. "I suppose I could sort another box of my father's papers."

Memories of Rob were the last thing he wanted crowding his mind. "How about looking at a photo album of Amy as a baby?"

Her eyes sparkled with interest. "I'd love to."

He found the album in the big chest under the window, and they sat close, the album balanced on both their knees. He took her through the first few years of Amy's life. A time filled with sweet, safe memories. "Life seemed so simple then. I knew Mom's heart wasn't strong, but it seemed she'd survived the pregnancy and delivery and regained her strength. I guess I didn't want to believe otherwise."

"Of course you didn't. Why let fears rob you of enjoying the present?"

"That's your philosophy, isn't it?"

She looked thoughtful a moment. "I suppose it is." She regarded him seriously. "What's yours?"

He looked at the fire. "I don't think I've ever thought about it, but I suppose I'd more likely want to hunker down and pull everything I cared about close to me and hang on."

She nodded slowly, as if she understood his statement. And if she did, she saw more clearly than he. "And shut out everything else to make sure it doesn't upset your little world."

"You make me sound like a selfish kid clutching his stash of toys to his chest and refusing to let anyone play with him."

"No. Not like that. Your world sounds nice to me. A safe, secure place. But that isn't my world. Never has been. So I've learned to look outside myself and enjoy the journey." She tipped her head, her blue eyes flashing a bright reflection from the fire. "I don't see you as being selfish so much as protective of both those you love and your own heart."

"I'm responsible for my family. It's not something I take lightly."

"I'd have to be blind not to see that. But I think you shut your heart against risks." She shrugged. "But what do I know? I'm playing armchair psychologist. You probably have a serious love interest I'm unaware of."

He laughed at that. "Depends on what you mean by love interest. Mrs. Shaw, one of our neighbors, has a lovely daughter she's handpicked to be my bride."

He leaned closer at the way Darcy's eyes darkened. Was she jealous?

"No doubt a very suitable match."

He delighted in the way her mouth puckered as she spoke. "Absolutely," he agreed.

Her frown deepened.

He couldn't resist stringing her along. "She's ranch-born and raised. Can ride and rope with the best of them. She's the one who always needles the calves in the spring." Seeing her startled look, he explained. "She gives the calves their vaccinations. She's quick and efficient. I couldn't ask for better. On top of that, she's a very good teacher right here in Blissdale."

"A truly remarkable woman." Darcy sounded anything but impressed.

"Only one problem."

She looked suitably shocked. "The woman has a flaw?"

He shrugged. "Probably not. But I guess I do. I can only see her as one of the guys. I'm just not interested in her as a woman." He didn't have room in his life for any more women. He turned his attention back to the photo album. "Here's Amy's third birthday party."

They bent together to study the people in the pictures. Did she linger longer on the ones with Rob in them? Was she beginning to see he was a good father to both Blake and Amy? Again that question—why not with Darcy? What had gone wrong?

The next page held a picture he'd forgotten. His mother holding Amy as she opened gifts. The look on his mother's face said so much. Sad yet full of love and pride. She must have known then that she wouldn't be around to see Amy grow up. How had she been able to sit through this party and smile at everyone? How had he been so blind he hadn't seen it coming?

Because he'd purposely chosen to ignore the signs. He wanted to protect himself from the pain of acknowledging her failing health. Maybe it wasn't such a bad way to be. Shut out pain. Don't give it a chance to linger. Don't even give it an opportunity to visit.

Darcy chuckled at the picture of Amy ripping open presents. Her arm pressed against his, warm and soft. Her hand brushed his as she turned a page. He could let himself get interested in this woman. After all, she was fun and caring. But doing so meant doing exactly what he'd so firmly avoided for years—opening his heart to risk. Letting one more person into his world to be responsible for. And to face the chance of losing.

He wasn't prepared to do that. She'd be gone in a few more days, and he'd say good-bye without any cracks in his heart.

As the day grew long, Amy's temperature rose, and they kept busy sponging her. Aunt Betty, too, grew more miserable. She tried to get up to give her cat its needed shots but swayed so alarmingly Blake insisted she stay in bed. "We'll look after Missy."

Darcy held up her hands and grimaced. She turned away so Aunt Betty couldn't hear her and whispered, "You do it." So Blake gave the cat the needle.

Between caring for the sick humans and the cat, filling the kettle, making hot drinks, and serving soup, the day passed. Blake barely had time to look out the window and hoped his herd had found shelter and safety in some trees.

The gray light faded, and the room grew gloomy.

Amy and Aunt Betty refused to eat anything and settled into an uneasy sleep.

Blake and Darcy sat together on the couch as they enjoyed the last of the soup. The evening hours passed as they talked about growing up and school days.

He told Darcy he took all his schooling at Blissdale.

"The same school for twelve years? It's amazing. I went to at least that many schools."

"Why did you move so often?"

"Mom liked moving."

"You didn't mind?"

"I didn't know it wasn't normal until I was a teenager."

"Do you feel the same need to move all the time?"

"I haven't moved in three years if that means anything. I

guess I could see moving if there was a need, but just to move? Nah. Not for me."

"Where's your mom now?"

Darcy laughed. "Now that's the funny thing. She met a guy in California. She used to go there almost every winter for the beaches. Anyway, they married a couple of years ago, and she lives there. Hasn't moved once since she married him. Of course, they go on lots of trips, so I suppose that meets her need."

Blake tried to fit Rob into this constant moving scenario and failed. "I can't see Rob liking that sort of thing. He could hardly bring himself to leave the ranch for any reason."

"You don't have to tell me."

"I'm sorry. I didn't mean to remind you."

She sighed. "Not to worry. Remember my philosophy— enjoy what God gives—the present. Besides, why is it you can't accept I lost my father years ago? Why do you want me to go over it all again? Why is it so important to you?"

He considered her question. "Partly because I think you're avoiding the past but also because I think it isn't fair to Rob's memory that you keep dismissing him as if he died a long time ago. There had to be something more to his not going back to see you."

She stared into his eyes, her own eyes flashing. "Like I was such a terribly bad kid he just had to get away from me. Or my mom was a mean drunk."

"It doesn't seem as if your mother was like that." He studied her features. The narrow chin. Was it quivering? He touched her cheek. Smooth as a spring breeze and kissed by the warmth of the fire. He caught a strand of hair that drifted across her cheek and tucked it behind her pretty little ear. Everything about her was so soft. "One thing I'm certain of, it wasn't because of you. You have a sweet, generous nature. You enjoy life and help others enjoy it, too." Too bad he wouldn't be enjoying it long term. "Perhaps Rob meant for you to come here and learn what he was like. Perhaps it's God's plan for you, as well."

She studied him soberly. "I never thought of it like that." She suddenly smiled, and the tension in his neck eased. "Thank you for reminding me that God is in control."

eleven

Darcy woke next morning to the sun streaming across her face. She blinked, disoriented, then remembered where she was—sleeping on the couch in Blake's living room as they waited out the storm. Only the bright sunlight announced the storm had ended.

Aunt Betty coughed. Amy moaned. Darcy sat up and glanced over the back of the sofa. Blake sprawled out on the recliner, his arms hanging over the edges, his head tipped to one side. He'd have a sore neck when he woke. She could tuck her pillow under his head, but he'd wake up if she disturbed him. He needed his beauty sleep. Right. Like he needed the plague. He was the most handsome man she'd ever encountered. Those warm chocolate eyes seemed to treasure every word she said. *Whoa.* She jerked her thoughts back. Sure, he was good-looking and kind. But—

He sighed and turned toward her, and she forgot all her "buts." Last night something had shifted in her feelings toward him. And she knew the exact moment it happened—when he reminded her of God's hand in her life. She knew then, Blake was a man she could trust.

She slowly pushed aside her covers and eased to her feet, glancing at him, wishing he would waken and smile at her. Perhaps with his mind clouded with sleep he would let his guard down and see her for who she was.

Darcy stared into the glowing embers of the fire. Who was she, indeed? What a stupid thing to think. What you saw was what you got. Darcy. Nothing more. Nothing less. No pretense. She snickered softly. That's what came of too many late nights, sitting before a fire.

She pressed the heel of her hand to her forehead. She didn't dream. She just lived. Ignoring the deep ache behind her eyes, blaming it on the late night, she tiptoed over to Amy, touching her forehead to check for a fever. She didn't seem too warm. Tenderness filled her as she smiled down at her little sister. Her throat tightened. How did someone walk away from a child like this? Yet her father had walked away from her. And she would leave at the end of her two weeks. Not that she thought Amy would even notice Darcy's departure. She was surrounded by love and care.

"Is she okay?" Blake's whisper jarred through her thoughts. She jerked her gaze toward him. Yep. Eyes soft and filled with sleep-muffled thoughts. Her breath gave a little jerk at the way he smiled at her.

"Amy's okay?" he repeated.

She sucked in steadying air and scolded her imagination back to the corner. "I think her fever is gone."

He sat up and looked around. "The storm is over."

She smiled as he bounded from the chair and squinted out the window at the blinding sunlight. "Not as bad as it might have been."

She joined him. "It's beautiful." The landscape spread out like a clean white sheet, full of mounds of whipped cream with sharp peaks.

He grunted. "I guess I should be grateful for the moisture, but I'll just be glad if the cows and calves are safe."

Aunt Betty stirred and moaned.

Blake turned from the window. "How are you feeling?" he asked softly.

"Awful," she croaked.

Darcy hurried to make the older woman a hot drink and give her two acetaminophen tablets.

"Missy." She pointed toward the cat. Darcy hid her shudder.

"I'll do it." Blake gave the necessary shot.

He straightened, grinning as humming filled the room. "Power's on."

Soon the room filled with warmth from the furnace. Aunt Betty dragged herself from the couch. "I'm going to my bed. I don't want to be bothered until I'm over this." She shuffled to her room, mumbling, "I don't want to be bothered at all."

Amy sat up and rubbed her eyes. As soon as she saw the sunshine, she scrambled from under the covers and raced to the window for a glance, then shot for the back door. "I gotta check on my cats."

Blake caught her as she charged past. "You're not going out with that sore throat."

She struggled in his arms. "I got to see if the baby kittens are okay."

He carried her back to her tangled blankets. "I'll check on them. You have to stay inside until you're better."

"I'm better already."

"You're not going out today, and that's final."

Darcy turned to hide a smile as Amy dropped her crossed arms over her chest in a defiant gesture.

Already Blake headed for the door. "I'll have to shovel the snow."

Darcy made breakfast and coffee, glancing out often to watch Blake steadily tossing scoops of snow over his shoulder. She knew from the way the snow clung to the shovel and landed in lumps that it was heavy and wet, but he worked until he had the sidewalk and driveway cleared, then left the shovel in a snowbank and headed toward the barn.

A few minutes later he stomped into the house.

Amy raced toward him. "Are they okay?"

"All cats accounted for. I fed them and gave them water." Amy sighed loudly. Blake smiled across at Darcy. "I checked on your house. Everything's A-OK."

"I made breakfast." She loved cooking and often made meals for her friends, but there was something cozy and special about making it for Blake and Amy. *Stop playing house,* she warned herself.

"Great." He helped himself to the bacon and eggs. "Don't tell anyone I said so," he whispered to Amy, "but this is a nice break from Aunt Betty's cooking."

Amy nodded. "Darcy should cook for us all the time."

Darcy sent her little sister a suspicious look. Had Darcy's thoughts developed a neon sign over her head? She forced herself to keep her gaze on Amy, afraid her expression would reveal more than she wanted. She well knew the distinction between fantasy and reality. And would never make the mistake of confusing the two.

Blake sighed. "We can't keep her just to cook for us. Besides, she has to go back to Seattle in a few days."

"Aww," Amy protested. "Why don't you ask her to stay?"

Darcy stole a glimpse of Blake twitching uncomfortably at Amy's suggestions. Poor man. She'd have to rescue him. "It's not that easy, Amy."

"Why not?" she demanded. "Aren't you big enough to do what you want? When I get big I'll do what I want." Her scowl dared anyone to argue.

Darcy laughed. "I guess I'm not big enough yet. I still have to do things I don't want to."

Amy wasn't buying it. "I won't when I grow up."

Darcy finally allowed herself to look at Blake, seeing her amusement reflected in his eyes.

"Good luck, little sister," he said.

At least they didn't return to discussing Darcy's ability to stay. If she were asked. . .

She knew no one but Amy would ask.

Blake lingered over his coffee as Darcy put the dishes in the washer and turned it on. She wiped the table and dried her hands on a towel. "I guess I'd better get back to my house." There didn't seem any more excuse to hang about.

Blake set his cup down. "I have to go check on the herd."

"What about Amy?" Darcy asked. "Aunt Betty isn't going to be able to supervise her."

Amy did her "mad" routine—crossing her arms and jerking them across her chest. "I don't need Aunt Betty to look after me."

Blake appeared thoughtful. "Don't worry. Aunt Betty will hear her if she's into anything."

Darcy had her doubts. She'd seen enough of Amy wandering around on her own. Of course, she realized children needed less supervision on a ranch than in the city, but it still felt a little scary.

"I'll just hang around until you're back. I have one more box to sort out anyway."

Amy bounced forward. "Will you make lunch?"

"Do you want me to?" Darcy looked at Blake.

"I can't ask you to do that. It's not your job." But his eyes said yes.

Her smile came from a roped-off area behind her heart. "I don't mind. I like cooking." And they needed her. It filled her with intermingling thoughts of belonging, being appreciated, and a trickle of fear and caution against letting those feelings out to play.

Blake nodded. "If you're sure?"

"I am."

Amy whooped. "I want. . . " She paused. "I want. . . " She sent a blank look toward Blake. "What do I like?"

His eyes danced with mischief. "Macaroni and cheese?"

She crossed her arms. "Not macaroni and cheese." She leaned toward her brother. "Tell me what I like besides mashed potatoes and gravy and homemade soup." She smacked her lips.

Darcy laughed. "You hardly tasted the soup I made."

"Yes, I did. It was good."

Blake ruffled Amy's hair. "Why don't you let Darcy decide what she wants to make? I'm sure you'll like it."

Amy nodded so hard her hair tossed over her head. "I know I will."

Darcy decided she would spend time with Amy, showing her some girlish fun before she tackled the last box of papers.

As soon as Blake left, she ran a bubble bath. She scrubbed Amy's hair until it glistened like bottled sunshine and blew it dry, curling the ends into a sweet flip. She found a brand-new pair of green cords in the back of the closet. "Where did these come from?"

Amy shrugged. "I think someone gave them to me."

Darcy dug further and found a matching green sweater. "These are really cute. Why don't you put them on?"

As soon as Amy was dressed, Darcy led her to a mirror. Amy stared at her reflection. "I'm pretty, aren't I?"

Darcy hugged her hard. "You're beautiful."

Amy returned to the mirror, pirouetting and admiring herself. Darcy wondered if she'd created a vain monster. But Amy's gaze shifted to her pile of stuffed toys, and she skipped over to pick them up and talk to them as she arranged them on her bed.

"I'm going downstairs to the office. I'll be there if you need me." Amy was so engrossed in her make-believe that Darcy wondered if she even noticed her leave.

She didn't want to go back in the farm office. She felt as if her emotions had been dragged along on the storm's wind—battered and rearranged until she hardly knew what to think anymore. If she let herself, she could spin a whole imaginary world where she became an integral part of life on the ranch. A partner to Blake, his caring what she thought of various things. Really and truly joint guardians of Amy.

Enough make-believe. The sooner she finished the last box, the better.

She paused at the office door, listening to Amy's murmurs overhead. For two cents she'd go play with her little sister. But then this job would still be hanging over her. She might as well do it.

This box contained letters. She hoped they were all farm related, but it took her about five minutes to realize she couldn't be so lucky. There were letters from Blake's mom, Kathy, which she set aside for Blake to deal with. There were birthday cards from Kathy and Blake and various aunts and uncles. Again she set these aside for Blake. He might want to keep them for sentimental reasons.

She saw an envelope with her mother's writing on it and grabbed it. What would her mother have to say to the man who had abandoned both of them for ranch life? She pulled out a card and stared at a mountain scene, then flipped it open. It said only "new address" and gave a house and street number. Darcy didn't remember that address. She studied the postmark and did some math. She'd only been six at the time. Had her mother sent him a notice of every address change? If so, she should find the evidence in this box. She pulled out a stack of cards held with elastic. More address-change cards. She flipped through them. One every six months or so for several years, and then about fifteen years ago they ended. She tapped the stack with a fingertip. Odd. Had her mother stopped letting her father know when they moved? Why? Was this the reason he had never contacted her? But all he had to do was call information for a number. But when had her mother started getting an unlisted number? She couldn't remember. Only that she'd done so after an ex-boyfriend started to hassle her.

She tossed the stack in the garbage and continued to sort through the contents of the box. She pulled out an envelope with her own writing on it. Without looking, she knew it contained the invitation to her graduation. She'd sent two tickets, thinking how generous she was to include the second wife. She could still imagine the taste of the glue on the envelope as she'd licked it, her hands trembling. Would he come to share this important occasion with her? She'd clutched the reply envelope to her chest when it arrived and carried it to her room where she put it on the bedside table and stared at it for a long time before she could bring herself to open it.

The response was yes. She remembered how she'd kissed the official card with only a check mark by the word, as hot tears flooded her eyes.

But neither of them showed up. And she'd never spoken to him or contacted him again.

She pulled the two embossed invitations from the envelope and ran her fingers along the printing.

It was seven years ago. It no longer had any power to sting. *Please, God. Help me not to let those long-ago feelings return. I've given them to You. They can no longer hurt me.* But she couldn't keep back the pain of that day. Her throat closed off. Her eyes stung. He'd never called or offered an explanation. A tiny memory plucked at her thoughts. Hadn't Mom said he'd called? Something about his wife being very ill. But she'd shut her mind to the excuses. And refused the calls from him until they no longer came.

A mental abacus clicked in her brain.

Seven years ago.

Amy was six. That meant—was Kathy pregnant with her at the time? Blake had said they'd discovered her weak heart when she got pregnant. Was it the reason they hadn't come?

She shoved the invitation back in the envelope and tossed it in the garbage. She wouldn't allow herself this torture— looking for reasons. Hoping for something to explain her father's absence. Besides, it would explain only one event.

Where had he been the previous twelve years? Why hadn't he called or visited or sent a card on her birthday?

Why was she letting herself get worked up about the past?

She dug further into the box. No more address-change notices. Nothing that gave her the slightest clue about what had taken her father so completely away from her.

Not that she was looking for it. She was only sorting old letters.

The box almost empty, she pulled out a folded letter and opened the three pages. She hadn't seen this dark bold scrawl before. She flipped the last page and read the signature. Rob Hagen. She lowered the pages and stared out the window, blinking from the glisten of the sun on snow. The eaves dripped. Blake's footprints filled with water.

She swallowed hard and looked at the pages in her hand. Her father had written this letter. Maybe it had been meant for her. She checked the first page. *Dear Kathy.*

What did she expect? A reasonable explanation?

The letter wasn't hers. She piled it with Blake's stuff.

A few more scraps of paper and the box was empty.

Darcy stood in front of the window, hugging her arms around her. Despite what she kept telling Blake, she'd been secretly clinging to the hope of something more. She hadn't found it.

Unless. . .

twelve

She turned back to the desk.

No. The letter wasn't hers.

But Blake gave her permission to sort through everything and decide what to do with it.

She reached for the letter.

The first page described the business trip that took her father away from the ranch for a week. The second page asked about the ranch as if he couldn't wait for the week to end so he could get back and discover for himself.

The third page began, "Kathy, you asked me to be certain before I told you again that I love you. I am more certain than ever. And I hope to convince you when I get back, but in the meantime let me try to make you see just how much you mean to me. On the ranch I have found a peace and contentment I've never before known. I'd be the first to admit that something about the land calms me. The rolling hills, the sunshine at noon, the distant mountains like guardians—"

Darcy stopped reading to press her finger to the bridge of her nose. She, too, felt calmness and peace as she gazed at the landscape. She could understand how her father would feel pulled to it. She continued to read.

"And I love the ranch, the demands of the work, the pride I feel in knowing I had a part in bringing it back from the edge of bankruptcy."

Darcy smiled through the sheen of tears, proud to know her father had been so devoted to a good cause.

"But those are not the things that matter most. It is you who have helped me heal, enabled me to get past my anger to this place of peace. Your love has made me whole again. I resent each moment I am away from you. I want to be able to see your smile every morning, feel your arms around me every night, see you smile when I tell you day after day until we're both old and gray how much I love you. Kathy, you are everything to me. Without you I am empty and aimless. Thank you for loving me when I was unlovable, for showing me the way back to myself, for believing in me even when I didn't. For showing me that God loved me. I will never leave you."

Darcy sighed as she finished the letter. Had her father ever loved her mother like this? She tried to remember them together, but nothing came. Was she too young to have memories, or had she blocked them from her mind? She closed her eyes and breathed slowly, calming herself, letting herself go deep into her memories. She wasn't sure, but she thought she saw them arguing. Had her father run from a tumultuous relationship with her mother to this peaceful haven with Kathy?

If so, she could forgive him. At least for ending his first marriage.

She didn't know if she could forgive him for leaving her.

Forgiveness?

She spun around to the brightness of the window. She'd already forgiven him. It was over and done with. Yes, a little explanation would be nice, but forgiveness was unnecessary.

"*Yes,*" the deep, calm voice within her said, "*you need to forgive him for abandoning you. And choosing Blake.*"

What he did was unforgivable.

She leaned her head against the window frame, remembering something a friend shared from going to a series of workshops after her divorce. "*Unforgiveness is like drinking poison and expecting our enemy to die.*"

But how could she let it go when there was no explanation?

It was easier to cover it over and ignore it.

"It will never go away if you do that. You will always be haunted by feelings of unworthiness even though you know you are precious in God's sight."

Unworthiness. Where had that come from? This was getting way too weird. Besides, it was time to prepare lunch.

She hurried from the room as if chased by a hundred voices.

She made a Mexican chef salad for lunch.

Blake rushed in, soaked to the skin, and dashed upstairs to change before he ate. "This is good," he murmured. "Can you watch Amy this afternoon? I have to find the rest of my cows."

"What happened to them?"

"They moved with the storm. I expect I'll find them bunched up in some trees, but I won't be able to relax until I find them all safe and sound."

"Amy will be all right with me. Aunt Betty seems content to sleep."

"Thanks." And he was gone before she could offer him dessert. Which was fine because she only had ice cream and a can of fruit salad from the storeroom downstairs.

❧

All the cows and calves finally accounted for, Blake could go home, his mind at ease.

He hated leaving Darcy at the house all day. Not, he was honest enough to admit, because he didn't want her there, but because he wanted to be there with her.

He'd make it up to her with the new video Norma Shaw had given him a few days ago. A chick flick. No doubt she'd planned for him to ask her daughter, Jeannie, to watch it with him. But he didn't have the time and certainly not the inclination. The idea of watching it with Darcy, however, made him forget work.

He jerked the truck into park and jumped out. Halfway across the yard he smelled roast beef, and his taste buds urged him to pick up the pace. He forced himself to slow to a gentle stroll so he wouldn't race into the house, panting and drooling like a starved man.

Cinnamon and apple aromas joined the beef smell as he opened the door. Amy raced over. "I like roast beef and apple pie."

Blake swung her up in his arms. "Me, too, squirt."

He met Darcy's gaze across the kitchen and winked. "We're a shameless pair when it comes to food."

Her eyes darkened to stormy blue, and his heart took off like a cow headed for new pasture. He forced himself to wait until after they'd eaten and Amy had wandered away to ask the question burning in his brain. "Why don't you stay and watch a movie with me tonight?" At the startled look in her eyes, he added, "I owe you for watching Amy."

She frowned. "She's my sister, too. And I'm joint guardian."

What would it be like if she stayed? Blake pushed away the idea. It was stupid to set himself up to be hurt. All he wanted was an enjoyable evening with her. He smiled what he hoped was his more powerful smile. "A nice, quiet evening. . .just the two of us. It might be fun."

She squinted and tilted her head. "Is this a date?"

"Almost. A movie date at home. I might even be able to scare up some popcorn and old licorice."

She laughed. His heart did a quick two-step as mischief flashed across her eyes. "An action adventure with lots of killing?" she asked suspiciously.

"Nope. A chick flick." He named the movie. "Have you seen it?"

She shook her head and studied him through narrowed eyes. "You're asking me to watch a romantic comedy with you?"

He nodded.

She let out a long, deep sigh. "I've been wanting to see that movie." She glanced at her watch. "It's a date, but I want to have a shower and change my clothes." She wrinkled her nose as if she smelled bad.

He could tell her she didn't. "Go ahead while I put Amy to bed."

She spun around and headed for the door, pausing to grab the old coat off the hook and slide her feet into her boots. He watched her puddle through the slush to her house, her shoelaces trailing in the water, and then he called Amy and got her into bed.

❧

He set up the movie, then made popcorn. He'd given himself several pep talks and warnings. *Be careful. Remember she'll be gone in a few days. Don't be begging for hurt and disappointment.* But surely he could enjoy an evening with her and still protect his emotions.

He knew the minute she opened the door. The soft gentle smell of spring rain wafted over him. A good clean scent.

He turned slowly. She stood uncertainly in the doorway, a fairy-tale princess in a luminescent pink shirt and white pants. Her dark hair shone as if it carried its own secret supply of diamonds. She wore it loose about her shoulders. "You look good," he murmured, his voice hoarse.

"So do you," she whispered, and he was glad he'd showered, shaved, and changed into black jeans and a black T-shirt. He reached for her hand and pulled her to his side as he led her into the living room. He'd pulled the love seat around to face the TV, and he settled her there.

"Can I offer you something to drink? Coffee, tea, a soft drink?"

"I'll have soda."

He opened two cans of soda, put the popcorn on the coffee table, and turned on the movie. It was the typical chick flick sort of thing with lots of girl-guy stuff, but she twisted her hands in her lap and sighed as if the plot didn't interest her.

Finally, he paused the movie. "What's wrong?"

"I keep thinking of something I found this afternoon."

He managed to mumble, "What?"

"A letter my father wrote to your mother."

"Something significant?" He could hardly resent this intrusion into their date. It was what he'd hoped for when he gave her the task.

She shrugged. "Maybe. I'll get it."

He stretched his arms across the back of the love seat and stared at the TV screen.

She brought a letter and handed it to him. "I probably shouldn't have read it, but I was curious."

"Not a problem." He skimmed the pages. "It sounds like Rob." He didn't know where she was going with this.

"You were right. I need some answers."

He could have pointed out it was a little late to be looking but held his tongue. "Did you find them in this?"

"Some clues. More clues here." She held up a bundle secured with a rubber band. "Address-change cards from my mother. The most recent is fifteen years ago."

His mental skills were good enough to do the math. "That's when Rob married Mom."

She nodded. "I know." She sat beside him, the cards in her lap. "If only. . ."

He pulled her close, and she rested against his shoulder, her fingers caressing the edges of the cards.

"I never realized how important it is for me to understand what happened. But I suppose it's too late."

He squeezed her shoulder, feeling her sadness, wishing he could ease it. "You could talk to Gene."

"The lawyer?"

"Maybe Rob said something to him."

She leaned forward, turning to grin at him. "Excellent idea. Why didn't I think of it?"

Because you need me. Out loud he said, "You probably would have." He almost wished he hadn't mentioned it because she sprang to her feet and crossed to the window, staring out into the dark. "I'll phone first thing in the morning and make an appointment." She headed for the door as if anxious to make the next day come faster.

He followed her. "I hope you find the answers you need."

"Thanks for the movie and the suggestion." Her eyes glowed with excitement. Unfortunately, he was pretty sure it was over visiting the lawyer, not over the evening she'd spent in Blake's company. But he was glad. He'd prayed she'd find the healing she needed.

&.

Darcy parked beside her house and sat staring out the window. Blake must have been watching for her return because he strode across the yard. She waited until he was beside her car before she climbed out.

"How'd it go?" he asked, searching her face.

She shrugged. "So-so."

"Well, what did he say?" He touched her chin tenderly. "Was it awful?"

"No. Just confusing. He said my father said I'd know what Amy needed." She searched Blake's eyes. "I don't understand. How can I know what she needs? I don't even know what I need."

Blake gave her a soft, understanding smile. "Maybe you know more than you realize." He touched her cheek.

She jerked away and instantly wished she hadn't. "Now you're going to talk in riddles, too?" She tried to pull mental armor around her. This whole business was turning into an emotional quagmire. "I was very angry with my father for a long time. I couldn't help wondering why he didn't care about me. What was wrong with me? It could have made me an angry, rebellious teenager if I hadn't been rescued by a very kind Christian lady. I just don't want to rake through all that stuff again. I don't want to derail my life, if you know what I mean."

"I'm sure he cared for you."

"Really?" She made no attempt to disguise her sarcasm. "And your proof for this theory is what?"

"I just know Rob. He was loyal and loving and—"

"To you. Do you know how that makes me feel? That he could love another man's son more than his own daughter?"

Blake jerked back as if she'd slapped him. "Maybe he just got tired of trying."

She recoiled. "As if I wasn't worth the effort?"

He reached for her. "No. I didn't mean it like that. I don't think that. You are a wonderful person, well worth knowing." He pulled her into his arms. At first she resisted his attempt to pull her close. But her need for comfort overcame her caution, and she let him cradle her to his chest. She could find peace in this man's arms. She'd seen how loyal and protective and caring he was.

"You know how I thought the world of Rob, but I confess he acted as if he had no past. Maybe he couldn't face whatever was back there. You have to see it was his failure, not yours, that kept you apart."

"It was my failure, too. I shut him out." His arm tightened around her as she shuddered. "I've never admitted it before, but I made it impossible for him to contact me after graduation."

He stroked her head and pressed his palm to her back.

Realizing they stood in the middle of the yard, she pulled away. "I just wish I could find some sort of closure."

"You will. You'll find a way. God will show you." He stroked her cheek. She grabbed his hand and clung to it.

She needed his reminder. Part of her wanted to drive away, push the whole thing into a dark corner, and forget about it entirely. But now that she'd cracked the door, there was no going back. She had to find peace with her past.

"I think I'll take Amy shopping in Blissdale."

"Good idea. I don't think Aunt Betty is ready to deal with her yet."

She found Amy, had her change into clean clothes, and did her hair.

"What are we going to buy?" Amy asked.

"Something new and pretty for you."

Amy looked interested. "Something pink?"

"Sounds about right."

Amy chatted all the way into town, pointing out neighbors and repeating everything she knew about them. As they neared the town, she showed Darcy her school. It was obvious she enjoyed her teacher and classmates.

The town had only two stores with children's clothing. Darcy let Amy choose several outfits and helped her try them on. She bought two pink outfits, some hair doodads, and a pair of glittering flip-flops Amy insisted on wearing. They had lunch at a little sandwich shop.

"Just like real ladies," Amy insisted.

Darcy laughed. Her little sister was a tomboy, raised in a man's world; yet she had deep feminine longings. Was that what her father meant when he said Darcy would know what Amy needed?

She didn't know. Perhaps she never would.

She knew only that she would miss Amy like crazy when she returned to Seattle. Their hours together had almost come to an end. Tomorrow Amy would return to school. The next day Darcy would leave.

Seeing a children's playground, she pulled over and spent an hour with Amy, storing up quality time and memories.

Finally, they had to call an end to the day and head back to the ranch. Darcy drove the length of the main street, then turned around.

Amy grew quiet as they passed the little white church. "Slow down," she said.

Darcy pulled to the curb. "What is it?"

Amy stared out the window. "That's the graveyard where Mommy and Daddy are. And Blake's daddy."

Darcy leaned over to look. A tidy little cemetery shaded by dark pines and poplars, in the pale green of early spring. "It looks nice." She studied the place with a deep ache.

"I go there to say good-bye. Sometimes we take flowers."

Darcy blinked. It was exactly what she needed. She'd take flowers and say good-bye. It would be her act of closure.

৯

The next morning Darcy delayed her trip to town until after nine so she could buy flowers. She ran an extra two miles in the morning just to deal with her nervous energy, pausing frequently to look around at the landscape. She loved the rolling hills, the fresh green of spring. She tipped her head and listened as a bird sang. A meadowlark. The prettiest sound she'd ever heard.

She lengthened her stride as she turned toward home, eager to head to town. It was silly, she knew, but this trip beckoned like a royal visit.

She bought a large bouquet in a heavy vase at the local florist and made her way to the cemetery. Suddenly, not wanting to face her task, she wandered up and down the rows, reading the headstones. And then there it was: ROBERT JOHN HAGEN. His date of birth, his date of death. In italics, *HE LIVED WELL AND LEFT TOO SOON*. Blake must have picked out the inscription.

She set the vase on the cement pad under the headstone and knelt in the damp grass.

"Well, here I am," she whispered. Her words sighed away into soundlessness. She remained motionless, wondering what she expected. She rested in confidence that God would reveal it. Bits and pieces drifted through her mind. Her father's smile. His flashing eyes. She couldn't say if they were from her memories or from the photos she'd seen in Blake's album. Or even seeing Amy and recognizing his resemblance in her.

He said he'd found peace here. Something he wouldn't have found with Mom. She moved too often for anyone to have a chance to unpack, let alone settle down and enjoy the surroundings.

Her father and mother had been unsuited for each other. Her mother simply wandered away too often, too far.

Darcy delved down into her feelings. She'd felt totally betrayed when he failed to come to her graduation. Now she knew it was because Kathy was pregnant with Amy and struggling with her failing heart.

"I forgive you," she whispered. "I understand there were more important things. And thank you for putting Amy first. She's precious."

She sat back on her heels. Then he got cancer. From what Blake said, he deteriorated quickly. No doubt he poured all his energy into spending time with Amy, helping her cope. Blake said her father had tried to find Darcy. Couldn't. Ran out of time and energy. Blake had been angry about that.

"You did well," she whispered. "Amy is going to be okay."

Again she sat in silence. Birds serenaded from the trees. The whole place seemed bathed with peace.

Her father had found his peace here. He'd found love and acceptance. She was glad he'd found what he needed.

"Good-bye," she whispered. "I wish I'd forgiven you long ago so we could have enjoyed some time together. Thank you for giving me the house and making sure I got to meet Amy."

She paused. "And Blake. I understand why you loved him. He is so kind and steady."

Her father found what he needed here. So had she. She'd

found her peace. She'd found a little sister. She'd found a man whom—

A man she could love?

She loved Blake. She let the idea slide through her, like a healing balm.

She chuckled softly. "Did you know this would happen?"

She arranged the flowers a little, then pushed to her feet. "I don't think I'll find the happy-ever-after life you did." Blake wanted no more emotional risks in his life. She understood that. It hurt to love, knowing you might lose the one you loved.

She stood in front of the headstone for a long time. Finally, sighing, she turned away. Tomorrow she had to head back to Seattle. But she wasn't walking away from everything she'd found here.

thirteen

"Where's Amy?" Darcy asked Aunt Betty.

"Who knows? That child shouldn't be allowed to run helter-skelter all over the place. I keep telling Blake she should be confined to the house, or at least the yard. She has a very nice swing set and sandbox."

"I'll see if she's with her cats."

"That's another thing!" the older woman called after her. "Those cats are probably diseased! If she brings in something that infects Missy. . . !"

Darcy didn't hang about to see what Aunt Betty said. As far as Darcy was concerned, Aunt Betty's animal presented more of a disease risk than Amy's well-nourished, vigorous cats.

She found Amy in the supply room, singing to the baby kittens. Darcy settled down beside her.

For a while they talked about the kittens and how they'd grown. Amy told her what she'd named each of them.

"Amy," Darcy pulled her closer. "You remember I'm leaving tomorrow?"

Amy looked down, silent for a moment. "Do you have to go?"

" 'Fraid so. I have a job and responsibilities."

"I don't want you to go." Amy kept her face tipped down.

"I wish I didn't have to. But"—she squeezed Amy's little shoulders—"I promise I'll be back."

"Something might happen to you."

Darcy knew Amy had too much firsthand experience with loss to offer meaningless reassurances. Bad things did happen. "Amy, honey, it would have to be something really awful to keep me from coming back to see you."

Amy leaned her head against Darcy.

She had so many things she wanted to tell her; but her throat closed off, and for a moment she couldn't speak. She forced the tightness away. "I am so glad you're my little sister. I will see you every chance I get." She'd fly there for holidays. It was close enough that she could fly out for a weekend. "I want to know when you have something special going on. If it's on a weekend, I'll be here. And soon you'll be big enough to come and visit me. I'll take you to the ocean, and you can play in the water. We'll have lots of fun."

"I'll like the ocean, won't I?"

"Of course you will."

Amy faced Darcy, her lips quivering. "I'd sooner have you here every day than see the ocean."

Darcy pulled her little sister into her arms. "I'd like that, too." Hot tears coursed down her cheeks. If only she could stay. But she couldn't. She'd committed to the race. She had a job in Seattle. And she didn't belong here. Not in the way she wanted.

She spent the afternoon with Amy. She would have taken her home and cooked supper for her, but Aunt Betty already had macaroni bubbling on the stove.

"Time to get washed up," Aunt Betty told Amy. "Be sure to scrub really well. I don't want barn germs in here."

Amy wrinkled her nose, but at Darcy's warning look went to obey.

"Aunt Betty, would you tell Blake I'd like to see him after he's eaten?"

"Certainly."

She went home to prepare for the evening and to begin packing.

৵

By the time Blake arrived, she'd worked out the details of what she wanted to say.

She opened the door to his knock. He stood in the evening shadows, dressed in blue jeans and a navy plaid shirt, the sleeves rolled up to his elbows. He smiled, his dark eyes warm and watchful. She caught her breath as she acknowledged her love for him.

"You wanted to see me?"

The world seemed to hold still while she smiled at him. She would cherish this moment forever. "Come on in." She waved him toward the living room where she had put out icy drinks and fresh chocolate-chip cookies. "Help yourself." She followed him and chose a chair facing him, knowing if she sat beside him on the couch as he expected, she would forget her carefully rehearsed words.

He took several cookies and bit into one. "Good."

"Thanks." She waited until he sipped his drink. "I'm leaving tomorrow." He put his glass down and studied her. "But I'm not relinquishing my joint guardianship of Amy." She'd never once agreed to, though she knew Blake expected she would. "I think she needs me. We can arrange for her to stay with me during her vacation time." She rushed on, ignoring the way his expression grew hard and set. She didn't want him to say anything until she was finished. "I've changed my mind about selling my house, too. I want to keep it so I can visit as often as I like." She took a deep breath and waited. It was the first time she'd belonged anywhere, and she wasn't going to give it up.

He continued to stare at her. She was sure she could smell rubber burning as he assessed her words. "Oka–a–ay," he finally managed. "I guess I'm not surprised. But are you sure it's the best thing for Amy?"

"Maybe this is what my father intended—that I would have input into Amy's life. I just know I can't walk away from her. I care too much about her." She tried not to think how much she cared about Blake. She didn't dare let her mind go there. Foolishly she'd fallen in love with him. But she wouldn't let it destroy her. She was an expert at pushing away things that hurt.

"You've certainly made her vacation memorable for her." He smiled. "And for me."

She nodded. "It's been fun." She mentally shut a few more doors against the pain she knew she would endure when she drove away. More than anything, she wanted to belong here. More than just owning the house. She wanted to be part of the fabric of his life. But she didn't belong. She never had, and she never would.

"I'm glad you're not going to walk away without a backward look."

She knew then he'd expected she would. Had perhaps even been counting on it. "I'm sorry I never tried to mend things with my father, but I can't change the past. I'm forever grateful he found what he needed here with you and your mother and Amy. I can't resent that."

"But you're going back?"

She nodded. "Tomorrow. I have to. The run and everything."

"Of course. Amy will miss you."

"I'll phone and write. And I'll be back every chance I get. I'd like it if she could spend part of her vacation time with me." He hadn't refused. Nor had he agreed. The last thing she wanted was a tug-of-war over custody arrangements.

"It won't be the same as having you here."

She pressed her lips together. She closed her eyes and forced a long, slow breath into her lungs. Somewhere she had to find the strength to leave. And the grace to do it without breaking down and upsetting everyone. *Lord, I trust You to help me.*

"We'll miss you."

"You mean Amy?"

He leaned forward, his eyes dark. "I mean me. *I* will miss you." He reached for her hands. "Who am I trying to fool? I love you. Marry me. It would be the ideal solution for Amy."

He loved her? How awfully convenient to discover he was

in love just as she announced she intended to remain a part of Amy's life. How ironic he came up with this idea at the last minute. For a moment she seriously considered the offer. She could care for both Amy and Blake. She could see her sister every day. She could accept this very convenient offer and be a very convenient wife to a man she loved.

But she'd been shortchanging herself long enough. She was worthy of a heart-shattering, life-changing, world-altering love.

She withdrew her hands. "Blake, it's a very generous offer but one I have to refuse. I want to be more than a convenient solution to a problem." She stood, feeling an urgent need to put distance between them.

He rushed to her side. "Darcy, it's not like that."

She moved away. "I'm sure both you and Amy will settle into a nice little routine after I've gone, and you'll thank me for not taking you seriously."

He took a step toward her and then another.

She backed away until she ran into a wall.

He stopped, inches away, and studied her, his expression serious.

She could almost convince herself he looked sorrowful but knew she would only be transferring her own emotions.

"You've forgotten one small matter." He gently cupped her chin in his palm and slowly lowered his head.

When his lips touched hers, it was all she could do not to melt against him.

He lifted his head. "I love you."

"Funny you just discovered this."

He shrugged. "Call me slow. Or maybe cautious."

"It would be the best thing for Amy."

"Yes, it would."

"She'd never be torn between us."

"No, she wouldn't." His expression grew increasingly cautious.

She took a deep breath and found the strength she needed to push away from him. "Sorry. I'm not interested in a marriage of convenience."

"Me either." He stalked from the room, pausing at the door. "You're doing it again, Darcy."

"What am I doing?"

"You're pushing away love because you're afraid of getting hurt." He slowly closed the door behind him.

She sank to the couch. *No, Blake, I'm finally seeing that I'm worthy of real love, not just convenience.*

৵

That night she lay staring up at the ceiling, waiting in vain for sleep to come. If he loved her, why hadn't he said so earlier? Why now? It was just too coincidental.

Maybe he'd only discovered it. Her own discovery was new.

She stared into the darkness. Could it be. . . ? Was it possible? If he loved her, he would not let her leave tomorrow morning without trying again to convince her. She laughed softly in the darkness as she allowed herself to hope. To be loved by Blake. To be part of his life.

It was all she could do to remain in bed when she wanted to rush over, throw herself in his arms, and confess her own love.

Lord, is this why You brought me here? To heal the past, find a new beginning? If so, I thank You.

"I love you, Blake Thompson," she whispered into the dark.

৵

Blake sat in the office. What's a man to do? He finally comes to his senses and realizes his world revolves around a certain woman, and he tells her so only to have her refuse his offer. Generous. Convenient. Of course it was. But it was also honest.

He knew what to blame. Her honed defensiveness. She'd shut out her father. Afraid loving would mean rejection. She was doing the same with him. She couldn't let herself believe him. She was afraid to belong.

Well, she'd been wrong about her father. He *had* cared about her. He'd kept that old picture by his desk all those years.

He jerked upright so fast the chair creaked. He could prove her father loved her. Maybe that would make it possible for her to accept *his* love.

He opened the drawer where he'd dropped her picture days ago and smiled at her childish sweetness. He polished the frame on his shirtsleeve and set the picture in the middle of the desk.

Finally, smiling, he climbed the stairs and fell into bed. Sleep came quickly and easily.

The next morning he headed for her house as soon as the first rays of light trickled over the horizon. She was already throwing things into her car.

When she saw him coming, she straightened, cocked one hip against the trunk, and crossed her arms to wait. He broke his stride at the way her mouth turned up and her eyes brightened. All welcoming and sweet. Had she changed her mind?

He closed the distance between them and stood staring down at her, unable to speak for the explosion of hope inside him. She smiled with the brightness of the sun coming over the horizon.

"I had to catch you before you left." His voice felt thick and heavy.

"Some special reason?" She didn't act surprised at his presence or his words.

"Were you expecting me?"

She lowered her gaze. "I—I'm not sure."

"I have something to show you." He held out the picture.

She took it and studied it. "This is me. Where did you find it?"

"Your father always kept it by his desk."

"But I was in there and never saw it."

"I shoved it in the drawer when you came. I was a little angry at the time." He gave her his best repentant smile.

"My father really kept it by his desk?"

"Always."

"And you never thought to tell me until now?"

He stepped back from the fierce look on her face.

She shook the picture at him. "You knew how much it would mean to me, but you never thought to tell me?"

This was not going the way he planned. "I forgot, but don't you see? You've always had a place here. A place in his heart. And now"—he held out his hands—"you have a place in my heart. Darcy, I love you."

She yanked open the car door and set the picture on the passenger seat. "One thing I've discovered here. I'm worth more than last-minute confessions and suddenly remembered revelations." She slid behind the steering wheel, slammed the door, and backed out of the yard, then paused and lowered her window. "I'll call Amy."

He managed to get in a few words before she closed the window and drove away. "Darcy, when are you going to stop running?"

&

Running, running, running. The pavement pounding beneath her feet. Blood pulsating through her veins. Driving every thought from her head.

Blake. Amy. Her father. It all seemed so convoluted. Why had her father left her the house and named her joint guardian of Amy?

He thought she would know what Amy needed.

She didn't even know what *she* needed.

Faster. Faster. Run. Don't think.

It was what she did best. Run until she no longer remembered anything.

"When are you going to stop running?" She almost faltered as Blake's words echoed through her mind.

She picked up her pace again, every piston drive of her legs striking home a truth. She was running away. She'd done it before, shutting her father out of her life rather than chance being rejected. And she'd missed knowing him.

Blake said he loved her, but she hadn't even given him a chance. Instead, here she was, trying to run away from her thoughts.

She knew what Amy needed. As clearly as a message written in letters across the sky. Amy needed to know those who loved her would be with her day in and day out, rejoicing in her accomplishments, comforting her in times of disappointment.

Maybe it was time for Darcy to stop running from her fear of abandonment and feelings of being unworthy. Maybe it was time to take a risk. What was the worst thing that could happen? Blake might change his mind. Better to have loved and lost than never to have loved at all.

She chuckled, knowing how the girls in the office always changed that saying to "Better to have loved a short man than never to have loved a tall." Usually remarked when the CEO wandered the halls. A short man but incredibly handsome and a real sweetheart. All the girls were more than half in love with him.

As she rounded the corner and headed down the home-stretch, she made up her mind. It was time to stop running and take a risk on the most important thing in her life—loving Blake.

She would quit her job and move to the ranch. She could either do contract work from home or get a job in Blissdale as an office manager. She might not get the same degree of responsibility she had now. That didn't matter. She could live on her savings for several months.

She would give her love for Blake a chance. And his love for her. Maybe he'd changed his mind. After all—

No, if he really loved her, he would welcome her back. No more running from her fears.

Darcy waved at Irene and pushed for one more burst of speed before she crossed the line.

Irene cheered. "Best time ever. You are going to take this race for sure, girl."

Darcy took the towel Irene offered and wiped her face as she paced in place, cooling off. "Two more days."

"I've never seen you work so hard. It's like you're trying to escape a horde of demons."

They headed for the showers. "Maybe I have been, but no more." She told Irene her plan. Her friend hugged her.

"Good for you. You deserve every bit of happiness you can find."

fourteen

"Why'd you let her go?" Amy demanded.

Blake sighed. Amy had been difficult since Darcy left. Not that he could blame her for feeling out of sorts. His own patience had taken a beating these past few days. "She had to go. You know that."

"You could have stopped her. You could have made her stay."

"Honey, she's a grown-up. She has to decide to do things on her own." He'd known she would leave. From the beginning he'd expected it. After all, look at her record.

"She wanted to stay, but you wouldn't let her."

"No, Amy. That's not true."

Amy crossed her arms over her chest and glowered. "You said something to her. I know you did. You were mean."

"No, Amy. I asked her to stay, and she wouldn't."

"I don't believe you."

Amy stalked away. Blake considered following her, but he understood her need to blame someone or something for Darcy's departure. Who did he blame? Himself, Darcy, her past, her fears. Sighing deeply, he headed for the office, the only place he could find peace lately. He tried to convince himself it wasn't because he caught hints of her scent or imagined her standing at the window or sitting in the chair.

Amy was wrong. He'd tried to convince Darcy to stay. He'd said he loved her. What more could he do?

He could have told her sooner. Why did he wait until she was leaving so it looked just a little too convenient?

Because he'd been too busy trying to protect himself.

From what?

From risk. From hurt. He knew firsthand how much it hurt to lose a loved one. And in his mixed-up way of thinking he figured if he didn't let himself love someone, he wouldn't have to deal with that pain again. Trouble was, by protecting himself, he'd spoken too late; and he knew pain stronger, more intense, more mind-bending than the pain of losing Rob or his parents.

Because she wasn't gone—she was just out of reach.

Unless—

Lord, forgive me for being so blind. Help her to hear what I have to say. What I feel.

He overturned the chair as he sprang to his feet. "Aunt Betty! Amy!" he roared.

Aunt Betty called from the living room. "I'm in here."

He hurried into the room. "I'm going to Seattle to see Darcy."

That got her attention. She jerked her gaze from the TV. "So you've come to your senses finally?"

"What do you mean?"

"That girl loves you, and you let her go."

"I didn't—" Why was everyone blaming him? "She loves me? How do you know?"

She huffed. "I may be old, but even if I was half blind I could see it."

"She loves me?"

"Question is, do you love her?"

He grinned like the village idiot offered candy. "I do."

"Well, don't just stand there. Go find her and tell her." She turned back to the TV. "Are you taking Amy?"

"Taking me where?" Amy demanded.

"I'm going to see Darcy and try to persuade her to come back."

"I'm going, too." She pursed her lips.

He contemplated the idea. "It's a long drive, and I'm not

going to waste time."

She didn't flinch. "I'm going, too. Darcy said she'd show me the ocean."

Blake hadn't thought what he would do when he got there past hugging Darcy and telling her he loved her until she was thoroughly convinced. But a little vacation sounded ideal. He'd arrange for someone to do the chores so he could get away.

He and Darcy could wander the beaches hand in hand, visit some special restaurants. He could see all her favorite places, go to church with her, see how she lived.

"I'm going," Amy said again, more forcefully. "You might mess up."

Blake laughed. "Six years old and you already think I can't handle things because I'm male."

"Me and Darcy are sisters." She said it vehemently. "We understand each other."

Chuckling, he swung her into his arms. "I'm sure you do. Yes, you can come. Let's go pack."

They were on the road in an hour. He figured if he drove straight through the night they'd get there in time to catch her race.

❧

Blake rubbed his stinging eyes as he fought the city traffic. He hated city driving. Stop. Start. Avoid the crazies trying to gain a fraction of a second by lane hopping. Only today, he was one of the crazies.

He glanced at his watch. They would never make it in time for the start of her race, but with a little luck they'd catch the end.

Traffic had been slowed to a crawl coming through the mountains, thanks to an accident. He'd prayed for God to open up a way for him and was grateful for getting through safely.

Amy struggled awake. Once she saw they were in the city, she sat up and strained to see everything. "Is this Seattle?"

"Yes, it is."

"Where's the ocean? Where's Darcy?"

"Haven't found either one yet."

"Why not?"

He sighed. She said it as if he'd been responsible for the delays. "We'll be there soon." He'd managed to track down the address of the race. It was only a few blocks away.

He jerked to a halt at a red light. Four more blocks to go. His knuckles whitened on the steering wheel. How long did this run take? He had no idea.

The light changed, and he edged forward, was cut off, and slammed on the brakes again. He struggled to keep his frustration under control.

He screeched the tires as soon as the way cleared. He came to a barricade. "This must be it." A few people hung about but not the crowd he'd expected. He drove around the block until he found a parking spot. "Come on, Amy. Hurry up."

She struggled a moment with her seat belt, then joined him. He locked the vehicle and strode toward the race route, practically dragging Amy along. He saw a knot of people ahead and hurried to them.

"Is the race over?"

A pretty young woman nodded. "You missed it."

"Who won?"

"Darcy Hagen. She blew away the competition."

Blake grinned. "Way to go. Where is she?"

The woman looked Blake up and down. "Who wants to know?"

Amy bounced up and down. "I'm her sister."

The woman turned her gaze toward Amy and smiled slowly. "You look like her." She looked again at Blake and studied him.

"Any idea where I can find her?" Blake asked.

She shrugged.

Now what? He pulled out his cell and called Darcy's home number. *No answer.* He didn't want to drive to her apartment if she was around the race route somewhere.

"Come on. Let's ask around." He asked several people if they knew where he could find Darcy Hagen. Some gave him blank stares.

Another woman looked him up and down before she said, "She left."

Amy tugged on his hand. "Blake, I'm hungry."

"Okay." They might as well grab something.

He found a fast-food joint and ordered egg burgers for them. While Amy used the washroom, he called Darcy's number again. Still nothing but the machine.

"Where's Darcy?" Amy demanded as she joined him, revitalized by her breakfast and bathroom break.

"Let's find her apartment and see if she's there."

He pored over the map, figuring how to get from the restaurant to her address. A few minutes later he found the place and knocked on the door. No answer.

A woman wearing pants too tight for her bulging figure and a man's plaid shirt yanked open a door down the hall. "You looking for Miss Hagen? You're too late. She checked out this morning."

"Checked out?"

"Yup. Didn't give me a month's notice like she's supposed to, but she gave me the money, so what do I care?" The woman shut the door.

"Blake. Where's Darcy?"

"Honey, I don't know." Had she run? Afraid to take a chance on a relationship? "I guess we might as well go home."

"I want to see Darcy."

"Me, too. But we'll have to wait for her to contact us." He clung to Amy's hand. This little girl would surely be enough to bring her back to them.

"Can we see the ocean?"

"Sure." No reason to rush back only to stare aimlessly out the window, wondering when Darcy would contact them.

&

They spent two days in the city, then took their time on the return trip. Amy enjoyed herself, though Blake often caught a hint of sadness in her expression. "I miss Darcy," she confided every night as he prepared her for bed.

"I do, too, little sister. But she'll come back. I know she will." He had to believe it. And if she didn't, he would turn the world upside down until he found her. He would hire a private investigator. He would never stop looking. And when he found her, he would beg her to give him another chance. He would tell her every day, in every way he could, how much he loved her until she finally believed it.

It was midafternoon when they turned down the driveway to home.

Amy screeched.

Startled, Blake slammed on the brakes. "What's wrong?"

"Darcy! Darcy!" she squealed.

Blake followed her gaze. Darcy's car stood in the sunshine at the side of her house. A grin threatened to split his face in two. "She's been painting." The trim was bright pink.

He headed back to town.

"Where are you going? I want to see Darcy." Amy started to cry.

"Kid, you'll have to wait your turn. I get to see her first. And I'm going bearing gifts."

Amy slammed her crossed arms over her chest. "Why do you see her first? That's not fair."

"You already know she loves you. And she knows you love her. I want to convince her I love her, too."

Amy laughed. "I knew it. I just knew it."

"What exactly did you know?"

"That we would all be together, like a real family."

He hoped Amy was right.

He couldn't decide on flowers or candy, and in the end, with Amy offering her advice, he bought a large bouquet of mixed flowers. Roses just didn't seem right for Darcy, so he chose daisies and chrysanthemums and forget-me-nots. He bought a large heart-shaped box of chocolates, a wind catcher that twisted and danced, a lawn ornament of a girl smelling roses, and a coffee mug with the words LOVE MAKES THE WORLD GO ROUND written in large pink letters.

"I can't carry any more," he told Amy.

Amy allowed him to drop her off at their house without protest. She smiled and patted his arm. "Of course she loves you," she told him in a wise, grown-up voice.

"I hope you're right."

He drove to Darcy's house and parked beside her car. She turned from painting the trim around the kitchen window and, seeing who it was, put her brush on the paint tray and climbed down from the ladder.

She wore an old shirt of his he'd outgrown and left in the house. A slash of pink crossed her nose.

He grinned. His heart picked up speed. He slipped out of the truck and filled his arms with three of his gifts. "Welcome home. I brought you something."

"Thank you." She took the flowers, chocolates, and coffee mug, her expression uncertain. "Where were you?"

"I went to Seattle to convince you I truly love you. When I couldn't find you, we spent some time wandering around the city. We wanted to see your home."

"I decided to come back. No more running."

"You saved me from hunting you down."

She laughed. "Why would you do that?"

"Because I love you and I'm prepared to spend the rest of my life proving it."

She buried her nose in the flowers. "I should put these in water."

"Wait." He returned to the truck and took out his other two gifts. He put the lawn ornament beside the door and hooked the wind catcher on a nail by the window.

"What is all this?"

"I just want to show you how much I love you." He moved closer, admired her saucy little mouth, her fine eyebrows that arched upward in surprise, her big blue eyes watching, waiting. He touched the slash of pink on her nose. "I love you, Darcy Hagen. I need you. Not to take care of Amy but to fill the spot in my heart reserved for you. Nothing else matters to me as much as you. I'll sell the ranch if you don't want to live here. All that matters is we're together."

She pressed her fingers to his lips. "Don't you dare sell the ranch. I would never forgive you."

He caught her hand and kissed her fingertips. "I'm glad. I don't know any other life. Darcy, will you share my life with me? Please say yes and end my misery."

"Blake, I love you."

He cupped her face and kissed her gently. This kiss was different. It was two hearts becoming one.

He lifted his head to smile down at her. "You didn't answer my question."

A teasing light filled her eyes. "You haven't guessed? Blake, I will marry you. I will love you now and for always."

"Hurray!" Amy's shout pulled their gazes toward her, hiding around the corner of the house.

Blake shook his head and laughed. "You were supposed to wait."

"I couldn't."

"Come on." He and Darcy opened their arms to invite her into a three-cornered hug. For the first time in his life Blake felt complete and whole.

epilogue

Darcy's mother helped her adjust her veil, pulling the shimmering material back from a satin comb tucked into Darcy's hair. Darcy had opted for having her face uncovered. "I don't want to miss one thing today."

"You're beautiful," her mother whispered before she took her husband's arm and let the usher walk her down the aisle.

Darcy stood at the back of the church, out of sight of the guests but where she could see them. She'd insisted they marry in the church Blake had attended all his life. Her friends had come from Seattle. Mrs. R sat right behind Darcy's mom. The rest of the guests were people who had known Blake forever and whom Darcy was learning to know. She'd been accepted into the community so quickly it amazed her. They'd welcomed her with invitations to dinner or coffee or quick chats when they met in town. They'd thrown a nice bridal shower. She'd been surprised when Blake informed her it was for both men and women. It had turned into a wonderful time of hearing stories about Blake she was certain he'd never have told her on his own.

She sighed deeply, her heart full to overflowing.

"What's wrong?" Amy asked.

Darcy turned her attention to her little sister. "Everything is perfect." She adjusted the pretty tiara in Amy's hair. Bright bits of rhinestone fell in narrow ribbons from the tiara like raindrops in the blond hair. She and Amy had shopped together for all the bridal finery. The more time she spent with the little girl, the more she grew to love her.

The same with Blake.

"Are you ready?" she asked Amy.

Amy nodded, her eyes bright with excitement.

"Then let's go." The girls held hands as they stepped through the doors to the sounds of the wedding march. Darcy faltered just a tiny bit as she found Blake's eyes and read his love. He'd opened his heart to her, filled her thoughts with his adoration, made up for all the years she'd wondered why she didn't measure up.

"You make everything worthwhile," he said often. "I will never stop thanking God for you. And thanking Rob for arranging for us to meet."

Blake made her feel whole and adored.

She and Amy reached the front of the church. As they had practiced, Amy stepped in front of them while Darcy and Blake joined their hands. And then everything else faded into the background as she turned to Blake, her heart so full of love and gratitude she wasn't sure how to control it. When she saw the same love and gratitude reflected in Blake's eyes, she silently promised she would spend the rest of her life pouring out her love for him.

And then they exchanged vows and kissed amid the applause and approval of friends, family, and neighbors.

As they made their way to sign the register, Blake whispered for her ears only, "Our life together has just begun. Just think how much better it will get with practice and with God's help."

A Letter To Our Readers

Dear Reader:

In order that we might better contribute to your reading enjoyment, we would appreciate your taking a few minutes to respond to the following questions. We welcome your comments and read each form and letter we receive. When completed, please return to the following:

Fiction Editor
Heartsong Presents
PO Box 719
Uhrichsville, Ohio 44683

1. Did you enjoy reading *Darcy's Inheritance* by Linda Ford?
   ❏ Very much! I would like to see more books by this author!
   ❏ Moderately. I would have enjoyed it more if

   _____

   _____

   _____

2. Are you a member of **Heartsong Presents**? ❏ Yes ❏ No
   If no, where did you purchase this book? _____

   _____

3. How would you rate, on a scale from 1 (poor) to 5 (superior), the cover design? _____

4. On a scale from 1 (poor) to 10 (superior), please rate the following elements.

   ____ Heroine   ____ Plot
   ____ Hero   ____ Inspirational theme
   ____ Setting   ____ Secondary characters

5. These characters were special because? _____
   _____
   _____

6. How has this book inspired your life? _____
   _____
   _____

7. What settings would you like to see covered in future
   Heartsong Presents books? _____
   _____
   _____

8. What are some inspirational themes you would like to see
   treated in future books? _____
   _____
   _____

9. Would you be interested in reading other **Heartsong
   Presents** titles? ❑ Yes ❑ No

10. Please check your age range:
       ❑ Under 18   ❑ 18-24
       ❑ 25-34   ❑ 35-45
       ❑ 46-55   ❑ Over 55

Name _____
Occupation _____
Address _____
City, State, Zip _____

Hearts♥ng

HEARTSONG PRESENTS TITLES AVAILABLE NOW:

Presents

Great Inspirational Romance at a Great Price!

Heartsong Presents books are inspirational romances in contemporary and historical settings, designed to give you an enjoyable, spirit-lifting reading experience. You can choose wonderfully written titles from some of today's best authors like Andrea Boeshaar, Wanda E. Brunstetter, Yvonne Lehman, Joyce Livingston, and many others.

When ordering quantities less than twelve, above titles are $2.97 each.
Not all titles may be available at time of order.

HEARTSONG
PRESENTS

If you love Christian romance...

$10.⁹⁹

You'll love Heartsong Presents' inspiring and faith-filled romances by today's very best Christian authors. . .DiAnn Mills, Wanda E. Brunstetter, and Yvonne Lehman, to mention a few!

When you join Heartsong Presents, you'll enjoy four brand-new, mass market, 176-page books—two contemporary and two historical—that will build you up in your faith when you discover God's role in every relationship you read about!

Mass Market 176 Pages

Imagine. . .four new romances every four weeks—with men and women like you who long to meet the one God has chosen as the love of their lives…all for the low price of $10.99 postpaid.

To join, simply visit www.heartsong presents.com or complete the coupon below and mail it to the address provided.

✂ -

YES! Sign me up for Heart♥ng!

NEW MEMBERSHIPS WILL BE SHIPPED IMMEDIATELY!
Send no money now. We'll bill you only $10.99 postpaid with your first shipment of four books. Or for faster action, call 1-740-922-7280.

NAME _____

ADDRESS_____

CITY_____ STATE _____ ZIP _____

MAIL TO: HEARTSONG PRESENTS, P.O. Box 721, Uhrichsville, Ohio 44683
or sign up at **WWW.HEARTSONGPRESENTS.COM**